The Lion and the Baron

December 1940

A Misfit Squadron Novella

Simon Brading

First published 2019

This edition published 2024

ISBN: 978-1-917470-03-2

PROLOGUE

The noise was the first thing he became aware of, through the unnatural fog clouding his mind. It was a very familiar sound, the drone of a steam-powered aircraft engine, and as a pilot it should have been comforting, but there was something not quite right about it, something that disturbed him.

All engines had their own note, their own distinct timbre, and someone like him, who had been around aircraft engines all their lives, was easily able to identify them just from hearing them.

Even in his dazed state it took him only a few seconds to recognise them.

The engines were Prussian. *Fischer-Bergs*. And that was bad news.

It wasn't bad because Prussian engines were bad, on the contrary, they were among the best, most efficient, steam-engines in the world.

It was bad because he was British and Britain was at war with the Prussian Empire.

The mists reached out for him, trying to drag him back down into the darkness, but something prickled at the corner of his mind, some feeling of urgency, of something left undone, of imminent danger for himself or for another, so he resisted, trying to claw his way back to the light.

Gradually he became aware of another sound over the near-constant drone of the engines, an occasional clinking noise, and with it came a delicious and distinctive smell, one that brought back memories of past visits to Munich and Berlin.

Curious, he opened his eyes, but immediately squeezed them shut again with a groan when the sudden light sent a bolt of pain to his temples.

'Guten Tag, Lord Drake! Are you hungry?'

The final vestiges of the drug-induced haze fled at the unwelcome voice and the memories of the last week came rushing painfully back.

CHAPTER 1

We'll talk when you get back.

Gwen's words echoed in Drake's head as he flew his Harridan through the freezing air above Northern Muscovy, his hands and feet automatically making the small adjustments required to hold formation with the flight leader while his mind was elsewhere.

He'd heard variations of the phrase from various women over the last five or six years and he knew that it could mean anything, from something wonderful, like a promise of delights, to something awful, like a scare or an ending. He also knew that the only way he would know for sure what it meant was to wait and hear what she said.

That hadn't stopped him from going through every possibility in his mind over and over, though, and he'd imagined himself alternately slapped and kissed more than a dozen times since takeoff. It was starting to get a bit repetitive, but for some reason he just couldn't stop.

He couldn't stop thinking about her.

Even though he'd heard that she'd joined Misfit Squadron and known they were going to be joining the mission to Muscovy, he hadn't been prepared for her to walk into the ready room on the *Arturo* and memories of childhood had come flooding back. At the same time, he'd felt intimidated by her new status as a hero of Britain and become quite flustered. He'd made something of a fool of himself and he felt his cheeks heating despite the cold as he remembered how he had tried to make more of his own role in her becoming a pilot, acting as if he were still that self-important 9 year-old.

He hadn't let that first disastrous encounter put him off and during the weeks they'd been at Vaenga he'd taken every opportunity to hint at how he felt about her. She hadn't taken much notice, or at least hadn't recognised his advances as such, and only had eyes for her American roommate, Kitty. Frustrated, he'd become more overt in his approaches, but to no avail.

Finally, things had come to a head at a party when, on impulse and after a couple of vodkas too many, he'd as good as proposed to her. Predictably, she hadn't leapt at the offer, but neither had she turned him down. Instead she had promised to think about it.

In hindsight that had probably been the best outcome he could have hoped for; he'd placed her on a pedestal during their years apart and idealised her until somehow over the years she'd become the love of his life, but she hadn't done the same - she'd even fallen in love with and married another man.

He was convinced that he could win her, though; he'd seen something in her eyes that morning, a gleam that made him think that he was going to like what she had to say.

We'll talk when you get back.

He smiled at the sweet sound of her voice in his mind and decided to replay one of the more pleasant daydreams, the one where Gwen accepted his proposal and they took a couple of days leave in a picturesque house near a frozen lake...

'Enemy in sight! Teacher flight, full emergency throttle. Now!'

Squadron Leader Rosaline Pemberton's voice came over the private frequency, startling Drake out of his reverie and he berated himself for having gotten so distracted in the middle of a combat zone. He slammed his throttle through the gate, then slotted lenses in place over his goggles and scanned the sky, twisting in his seat, trying to spot the enemy aircraft. He could find no sign of them and for the umpteenth time he lamented the fact that regulations stated he had to use the cheap RAC-issue lenses, wishing, as always, for his own Swiss-fabricated set.

He thumbed his transmit button. 'Two here. I don't see them, Leader.'

'Twelve o'clock low, Two. That damn fool Baryshnikov is going straight for them.'

While it was indeed Wolfpack Squadron's job to intercept incoming Prussian aircraft, that morning they were supposed to be on a training flight.

Under the watchful eyes of the instructors the thirteen Harridans had headed east, away from the front lines, to carry out basic manoeuvres so that the four pilots, who'd arrived only hours before, had a chance to get to know their new Harridans before being thrown into the fight. Since it was a training flight and not a combat sortie, Pemberton was in charge, and her orders had been very clear - in the unlikely event that an enemy should appear, Baryshnikov was to take his squadron to safety and not engage.

Drake wondered what the enemy were doing so far from any worthwhile targets, but when he looked in the direction Pemberton had indicated he was horrified to see the sun glinting on the river that marked the border with Norway and the front line - not only was Captain Sergei Baryshnikov contravening Pemberton's orders and moving to engage the enemy but, while Drake had been daydreaming about Gwen, the man had reversed course and deliberately gone looking for them.

There was a sharp crackle as Pemberton switched to the channel they shared with the Muscovites. 'Wolfpack Leader this is Teacher Leader, disengage, repeat, disengage and return to base.'

There was no answer, though, just silence, and Drake smiled wryly, knowing full well that the headstrong Baryshnikov was either ignoring her or too busy shouting at his pilots to take any notice.

They were much closer to the gaily-coloured Harridans of the Wolfpack now and Drake went cold when he finally saw what had gotten Pemberton in such a flap.

The aircraft that the Muscovites were rushing headlong to engage were bright red - it wasn't just any old Prussian squadron the Wolfpack were attacking, but the *Crimson Barons*, the best pilots the enemy had, equipped with the best aircraft. And the damn fool hadn't even kept his height advantage but had descended from their patrol height and led his men and women straight in at treetop level to where the Prussians were attacking the ground forces.

The result was utterly predictable and the three instructors were forced to watch, helpless, as the Muscovite Harridans began to fall from the sky, the new pilots, whose names Drake hadn't even had a chance to learn, the first to fall.

'What are we going to do, Skipper?' asked Betsy Howard, her uncertainty clear in her voice. Of the three, she was the most technically brilliant and was able to get the best out of even the worst student, but she lacked real combat experience, having been an instructor before the war and then kept off the front lines to continue her job.

Pemberton had a hard choice to make. Their orders from the Ministry for War were clear, they were not to engage the enemy while in Muscovy because their ability to train pilots was far more important to the war effort than the few kills they might make, but if they didn't do something before too long, there wouldn't be anybody left to train. Ordinarily, she was a real stickler for the rulebook, but Drake was fairly sure she wouldn't abandon pilots they were responsible for and allow them to be slaughtered.

A single glance across to Pemberton gave him all the confirmation he needed; the cold composure that had earned her the nickname *The Ice Queen* from her students in Britain was gone and in its place was a white hot fury, evident even beneath the breathing apparatus and goggles covering most of her face.

Pemberton answered Howard with a snarl. 'Bugger this for a lark! Teacher flight, pick your targets and engage. Let's hope the bastards are low on tension and ammo so we can get at least a few of these girls and boys home.'

The three Royal Aviation Corps pilots drifted apart as they swooped, giving each other room to manoeuvre while still maintaining an invisible thread between them - the instinct and understanding that weeks of working together had developed.

Straight away Drake saw his chance when two of the red machines crossed in front of him, chasing after the same Harridan, playing with it, supremely confident in the outcome. He banked after them, fully intending to disavow them of that conviction. He lined up on the leader of the pair and squeezed the trigger on his stick, giving the enemy aircraft a full three-second burst from his twelve machine guns. The immense recoil from the guns slowed his Harridan noticeably, but the effect on the Baron's *Blutsauger* was far more pronounced and it folded up as if it were made of paper and dropped like a stone.

He switched his aim to the other machine, but, lesson learnt, it jerked away from him and disengaged from the Muscovite aircraft. He turned to follow it, but tracers shot past his canopy and the Harridan lurched as something impacted on his right wing, tearing a large hole in it and obliterating the lion of the roundel. He threw the machine into desperate manoeuvres, spiralling down out of the sky until he was only feet above the canopy of the forest, then put the machine into a maximum rate turn, craning his head to look for his attacker.

There were two of them - two Blutsaugers had followed him down and were firmly stuck on his tail, one behind the other.

He held the turn, watching the relative angles and was relieved when he saw that the Harridan was out turning them. It was only by fifteen or twenty degrees per second, but that was more than enough to ensure not only his survival, but his victory. His vision narrowed with the G force and he shouted his annoyance at stupid regulations which prevented him from wearing the flightsuit his parents had bought him on his eighteenth birthday, the effort serving to force blood back into his head.

With each second that passed the two machines slowly traversed his canopy, seeming to move backwards as he gained on them. The worried faces of the two Prussian pilots stared back at him across the wide circle the three machines were describing in the air and he grinned in satisfaction, knowing he would be able to take at least one more of the Barons out of the fight and maybe the war.

The rearmost Prussian fighter swam lazily across his windscreen, approaching his sights, and he curled his finger around the trigger in anticipation.

The stick juddered under his hand, but it wasn't vibration from his guns and he swore as a series of huge holes appeared as if by magic on his wing, jerking him almost completely out of the turn with the heavy impact, and he flinched involuntarily as a third enemy aircraft screamed past him, almost close enough to touch.

This machine wasn't completely red, though; its nose was checked black.

Gruber.

Drake forgot about the two Blutsaugers in the face of the much greater threat and put his Harridan onto its other wing to pursue their leader, who was racing away at top speed only feet above the tree tops, the empty branches swirling and grasping in his wake.

Drake had been going relatively slowly during the turn so Gruber pulled away steadily at first, but with the Harridan's new Rentley-Joyce spring once more at full emergency unwind the gap soon stopped widening, then slowly began to close.

As Drake chased the red and black machine he kept his eyes roving around the sky, making sure that none of the other Barons were trying to get the drop on him, but they were all engaged with the instructors and what remained of the Wolfpack, who appeared to be holding their own a bit more.

The Harridan closed to extreme firing range and Drake smiled grimly as he moved his finger back over the trigger, but he didn't open fire; at that distance the streams of bullets from the machine guns would be converging and most, if not all, of the rounds would go to waste. He waited, biding his time as he crept slowly closer to Gruber's aircraft.

At six hundred yards he knew he was still beyond optimal firing distance, but he was getting impatient and he knew he had plenty of ammunition to spare so he took a deep breath to steady himself, then slowly applied pressure to the trigger, as if he were a sharpshooter.

In the same instant he fired, Gruber disappeared.

For a split second he was unsure what had happened, but then he saw that the endless sea of tall trees ended suddenly ahead at the river and realised that the Prussian aircraft had ducked behind them, gaining cover temporarily, moving so fast he had missed it in the space of a single blink. That wouldn't save Gruber, though, because when Drake reached the same point there would be nowhere left to hide and he would be an easy target.

It was less than a third of a mile to the cliffs at the edge of the river and Drake's Harridan covered it in only slightly more than a second, but when the last of the tall trees disappeared below him Gruber's machine was no longer in front of him, but already far away off to one side - the Prussian had known that his pursuer would lose sight of him momentarily and had taken the opportunity to throw his aircraft into an impossible turn that would have torn the wings off anything other than a biplane. Drake kicked his rudder to slew his Harridan and gave him a quick burst, but it was a futile gesture made out of frustration.

He knew there was no way he could match Gruber's manoeuvre, so he didn't even try and just went into a steep climb, substituting his greater speed for altitude to put him outside of Gruber's reach so that he could turn safely before coming back.

He used the opportunity to search the sky again, making sure nobody was waiting to pounce, but there was nothing except for the solid white of clouds. They had left the rest of the fight far behind. There was nobody to swing the balance in favour of either of the combatants.

He grinned and glanced at his instruments. His airspeed had come down considerably and it was almost time to turn back.

Although if Gruber had made his escape that would be no great loss...

Several heavy thuds shook the Harridan and he looked up in shock to find his rear view mirror filled with red and black checks.

'How in the...?'

That was all he could get out before the wing of his aircraft separated from its fuselage and he was slammed sideways. His straps brought him up short before his head could hit the canopy, but they dug into him painfully as the Harridan spun, plummeting towards the trees below.

He had only seconds to get out before he hit the ground and he fought to get to the canopy release, his arms many times heavier than they should be. With a supreme effort he found the latch and the glass shot back. It shattered as it slammed into the stops and showered him with glass, but he barely noticed because he was already struggling to undo the straps holding him to the Harridan.

One more second was all he needed.

He didn't have it.

We'll talk when you get back.

The last thought that crossed his mind as his aircraft hit the tops of the trees and began tumbling sickeningly was regret that he would never know what Gwen's words had meant.

CHAPTER 2

The afterlife was cold.

He remembered thinking that afterwards, a long time afterwards, because his next thought wiped that one out of his mind.

Ow.

Drake couldn't remember ever having been in so much pain before. Not when he'd fallen out of the big oak on the estate, nor when he'd been forced to land in a convent's wheat field and the sister superior had chased him with a stick for destroying a large part of their crop.

Not even when he'd seen Gwen with Kitty...

However unwelcome it was, though, at least the pain, told him he was alive.

He opened his eyes, wondering how he had survived and couldn't help but laugh, even though it hurt and made him gasp for breath.

The Harridan had a well-deserved reputation for being robust and forgiving of even the most inexperienced pilots. It wasn't nearly as skittish as the Spitsteam and would stay in the air well after sustaining damage that would have knocked the more temperamental aircraft out of the sky. Drake had seen Harridans make it home with half a wing missing or with very little in the way of tails and even when one of them did crash - like when the pilot was too injured to carry out a safe landing, or insisted on trying to put the aircraft down without using the undercarriage (something that happened far too often) - all was not lost and many pilots still survived even the worst prangs due to one special design feature, the *Hawking Cage*, a framework of reinforced metal around the cockpit which enclosed the pilot in a protective shell. (It also reportedly acted as a Faraday cage and protected the pilot against lightning, but Drake had never heard of anyone being silly enough to go up in a thunderstorm to test that hypothesis.)

Ironically, it was a young Gwenevere Hawking who had come up with that particular design innovation and it had undoubtedly saved his life that day because it looked like he was going to set a new record for how badly damaged an aircraft could be after hitting the ground and the pilot still be able to walk away; his Harridan was missing both wings, the airscrew and most of its nose, and all of its tail, leaving only a few scraps of Duralumin attached to the cockpit. Miraculously, and to his vast relief, the casing for the spring hadn't been damaged, or at least not catastrophically; of all aircraft crashes, damage to the spring was the biggest cause of pilot death - the razor sharp brass ribbon unravelling at great speed could rip through the metal fuselage with ease and did unspeakable damage to the much softer person within.

Unfortunately, he wasn't *technically* on the ground yet. He was stuck in the boughs of a tree, some twenty yards up. Thankfully, though, he was more or less the right way up, so he didn't have to worry about falling when he undid his straps - he'd heard of too many pilots flipping their aircraft on landing, surviving intact, then undoing their safety harness and breaking their necks.

However, he needed to assess how bad his injuries were before he could even think about how to get down. It was no use putting effort into climbing down only to bleed to death in the snow, if he was going to do that he might as well do it in the comfort of his cockpit while enjoying the brandy from his survival pack.

His arm was the main source of pain and the way it was bent half-way between his wrist and elbow told him quite clearly that it was broken, but a quick once over of the rest of his body surprisingly found nothing else serious, just a pretty big lump on his temple, a pounding headache and the expected bruises from being knocked around like the sparring partner of the heavyweight champion. He was extremely cold, though, and gently shivering, his thermals and greatcoat not quite adequate for the weather, but that was a comfort; he'd be more worried if he felt warm, because that would most likely mean hypothermia was setting in.

It was truly remarkable how lucky he had been, but there was one last piece of the puzzle to slot into place before he could truly celebrate - he had to work out where the hell he was and more importantly what side of the border he was on.

The Barons had been attacking the Muscovite ground troops, so the initial engagement had taken place over friendly territory, but he couldn't be sure if he'd crossed the border during the following fight and he had no idea which way he'd been heading when he'd climbed away after chasing Gruber back to the river.

With no way of knowing for sure which side of the lines he'd come down on, he decided not to risk anything. When he got out of the tree he would head east as stealthily as he could and hope for the best. If he ran into Muscovites he had been armed with a few phrases in Russian to stop them from shooting him and there was a patch on his flightsuit from Wolfpack squadron in case he mangled the phrases so badly as to be unrecognisable. If he ran into Prussians on the other hand... Well, he would have to deal with that eventuality as best he could.

A sudden violent bout of shivering reminded him of how cold he was and he realised that he had to get moving before he became too stiff to move.

He turned his attention to the straps holding him in his seat and a shudder, which had nothing to do with the temperature, ran though him when the clips popped out of the quick release wheel as soon as he touched it; it had been almost fully unlocked and if he'd managed to turn it just a fraction of an inch more he would have been unstrapped when the Harridan hit the trees.

He grinned grimly; the Dark Scythesman must be gnashing his teeth in his skull at being so narrowly cheated of his prize. Then again, he wasn't exactly out of the Scythesman's clutches yet; he still had to make it down to the ground.

Past tree-climbing adventures flashed through his mind and he grimaced when he realised just how many of them had ended in some mishap or other, even with two good arms, but it wasn't as if he had any choice in the matter; he couldn't stay where he was. At least, if he did fall, there was no annoying seven-year-old girl to laugh at his clumsiness.

He carefully slid his bad arm inside his greatcoat to keep it out of the way and stop him forgetfully trying to use it before pulling off his helmet and mask. He then unclipped the cushion-sized knapsack containing a survival kit from its place attached to his glidewings and slung it over his shoulder.

He stood, somewhat unsteadily, and peered over the side of the cockpit.

It was a daunting task and a hell of a long way down, but the trees were perfect for climbing with plenty of branches to choose from so, even one-handed, he was fairly confident of making it to the ground in one piece.

He swung a leg over the side of the cockpit and froze when the fuselage shifted below him, his weight upsetting its delicate balance. He waited for the worst to happen, but aside from a few creaks of frozen wood and the groan of already stressed metal twisting further, nothing did. For more than a minute after the noises died down he held still, reluctant to try his luck any further, but his muscles started to ache and he realised that he couldn't remain where he was, he was going to have to chance it.

He just gritted his teeth and leaned out to grasp a branch with his good hand, ignoring the renewed sounds of distress from his poor Harridan then, as smoothly as possible, stepped out, transferring his weight onto the nearest bough.

The luck that had kept him alive up till then ran out in that moment.

The branch he had chosen to grab onto snapped and he lurched. His toe caught on the lip of the canopy and he fell forwards onto the bough. He hit it hard, knocking the wind out of him and sending a sharp pain through his broken arm. He clutched at it and for a second thought he was going to be alright, but then the fuselage shifted, settling into a new position and there was an ominous crack.

'Oh, sh...'

The words were ripped from him, along with his breath as the bough broke.

As he fell he hit branch after branch, sending him tumbling head over heels, and he screamed as his arm was struck repeatedly. The world around him faded to a single white point in his vision, the pain receding with his consciousness, but then a cold shock and sudden deceleration as he hit a snow bank face down brought him rushing back.

He screamed again, but this time it was muffled by the snow that surrounded him and it filled his mouth when he drew in a ragged breath. He struggled onto his side, coughing out slush then panted through gritted teeth, fighting to retain consciousness. He kept his eyes squeezed shut, clutching his arm to him as the agony slowly subsided and his racing heart slowed.

When he was finally able to take normal breaths again he opened his eyes and it was then he noticed the high boots planted in the snow in front of him.

He looked up and found the blue eyes of a man in a grey and white camouflage snowsuit gazing down at him. He then took note of the very Prussian insignia on his shoulders and the rifle in his gloved hands, the barrel of which was dark and menacing and pointed directly at his head.

The man smiled and spoke in a very thick, very Prussian accent. 'Hello, Tommy. Thank you for dropping in.'

Drake grinned in return. 'What oh, Fritz! Is it time for tea?'

CHAPTER 3

There were four Prussian soldiers, one of the patrols that had been sent out to track the downed aircraft from the dogfight going on overhead, in search of survivors, both friend and foe. They had apparently been waiting for him to come down for a couple of hours, making bets on whether he was alive, how long it would take him to get down to the ground and whether he would make it in one piece. As they marched Drake between them they congratulated those of their number who had won, while commiserating with those who had lost, all the time making jokes at the expense of the "foolish Englishman" in German, never for one moment suspecting that Drake understood them. He had taken German for several years at Eton, then practised it on a Prussian girlfriend, Rebekka, while at university, but had decided not to let on that he spoke their language, thinking that they might reveal something he could use if they thought he didn't know what they were saying. Instead he just grinned at them like the fool they thought he was as he staggered along, trying to keep up a good pace through the snow so that he man behind him had as few excuses as possible to poke him in the spine with his rifle.

Every step he took sent shards of pain coursing through his body from his arm, no matter how tightly he held it to him, and his strength was fading fast, black dots coming to life in his vision and crowding in on him. It was all he could do to put one foot in front of another, which was why he missed the grey shadow detach itself from a tree and it wasn't until a fearful shout from one of the Prussians became a gurgling scream that he stumbled to a halt.

He turned slowly, wondering what he would encounter, and recoiled in shock at the gory tableau that the stark landscape had become.

The pristine snow that he had only just trudged past was stained a brilliant red in a wide circle and the Prussian soldiers who had been following him were now no more than four crumpled bundles of cloth. Standing over them, blood dripping into the snow from two wicked-looking knives, was a figure dressed in grey.

'What...? Who...? How...?' His mouth was forming the words before his brain, dulled by the cold and the pain was fully able to take in the details of the scene before him. He trailed off as he finally managed to look beyond the blood and see the light grey flightsuit and darker grey Muscovite parka the figure was wearing. It was a pilot and, by the patch that matched the one on his own flightsuit, one of the Wolfpack.

Dark blue eyes crinkled beneath the hood of the parka. 'Which of those questions would you like answered first, Lieutenant?' The voice was muffled by a scarf and the accent thick, but it was perfectly understandable and recognisably female.

'Huh? Oh, um... Who. I mean, who are you?'

A bloody hand, still clutching a knife, pulled down the scarf then pushed back the hood, revealing a young woman in her early twenties. Her blonde hair was pulled back into a severe ponytail, but many of the strands had escaped and framed her oval face in a way that wasn't unattractive. It wasn't a face he recognised, though, and he frowned.

She saw his expression and smiled. 'Praporshik Guseva, sir. Wolfpack Nine.' She nodded respectfully and drew herself up to something approximating attention, revealing that she was tall, only a couple of inches shorter than him.

One of the new recruits, thought Drake. That morning's flight would have been her first time ever in a Harridan and even the best pilot in the world would have been hard pressed to survive against the Barons in an unfamiliar machine. She had most likely been one of the first shot down.

'Um, and, er, how?' He gestured at the bodies with his good hand. 'How did you do this?'

She shrugged, as if to say that she didn't really know why he even needed to ask. 'They were stupid. They didn't expect enemies here behind their lines. Also, I was a hunter before the war - I know how to kill animals.'

Drake looked at the long blades in her hands, then down at the Prussians. Despite the amount of blood there was very little sign of violence, only cleanly slit throats or spreading patches of red on the backs of their snowsuits. The woman had wielded her weapons expertly, taking the men down with precise strikes before they could even think to bring their guns to bear. In Drake's limited experience it didn't so much seem the work of a hunter, but rather an assassin. Before he could question her on it, though, she threw her knives into the snow point first, then bent down and started searching the bodies, pulling out things and tossing them onto one of the few patches of clean snow. She worked efficiently and soon had a pile of items including food, water bottles, firelighters and spare clothing. She didn't take any of their rifles, though.

'What about the weapons? Shouldn't we take a gun?'

'If you want to carry one, be my guest, but if you use it we're as good as caught, because you will bring every Prussian in miles.' She plucked one of her knives from the snow and brandished it with a diabolically enthusiastic grin. 'My way is better.' The snow had removed the blood from the blade and it glinted in the weak winter sunlight filtering through the trees. If anything the knife looked more wicked clean than it had covered with blood and Drake swallowed as she gave it a last flourish before making it disappear somewhere among her clothes.

She bent again and stuffed the provisions into a backpack that she pilfered from one of the soldiers, then got to her feet. 'Come on, Lieutenant, we should go before these idiots are missed.'

She began to walk away, along the path the Prussians had brought Drake, back towards the crashed Harridan.

Drake glanced at the compass on his wrist and frowned when he saw she was going west, away from Muscovy. He called out to her, trying to keep his voice as low as possible. 'Guseva! The border is that way.' He pointed east.

The woman stopped and sighed in exasperation, dropping her head to her chest before turning back to him. 'Home may be that way, yes, but so is the entire Prussian army. Did you have some plan to get through them and across the border without being shot?'

Drake groaned inwardly, cursing his own stupidity. 'No.' He smiled sheepishly. 'Sorry, I'm not good at this kind of thing.'

The Muscovite rolled her eyes. 'So I see. Now shut up and walk.'

He chuckled. 'Yes, ma'am!'

She grinned at him, then started away again.

He trudged after her through the snow, but any energy that he'd recovered during the brief rest was soon gone and after less than an hour, when the mainly deciduous trees near the river had given way to evergreens, he finally stumbled and fell flat on his face, biting back a scream as the bones in his arm grated together sickeningly.

He must have blacked out again, because the next he knew, he was lying on frozen earth with a thick roof of evergreen needles only a few feet above him.

The woman's face appeared in his vision and glared at him accusingly. 'You're hurt. You didn't tell me you were hurt. Is it your head? You have a lump there, but it's no more than a child would get falling over.'

Drake grimaced and struggled to sit up. 'It's not my head, no - my wing's clipped.'

'Your wing? What does that mean?'

'My arm, Guseva. It's a way of...' Drake sighed, not quite up to the effort of explaining British expressions to the woman. 'Never mind. I have a broken arm.'

'Ah! I can look at it if you would permit?'

Drake shook his head. 'I don't think...'

'I trained as a nurse before the war, sir. Do not worry, I can help. And please, call me Tatiana.'

'Thank you, Tatiana.'

The woman chuckled softly. 'Do not thank me yet; there is nothing to dull the pain.'

'In my bag.'

The Prussians soldiers hadn't bothered taking Drake's knapsack from him and there was a small, but fairly comprehensive medical kit in it. He found it next to him and began fiddling with the clasp, trying to open it with one hand.

Tatiana watched him for a few moments then tutted, took the bag from him and opened it.

'There should be a tin with a red cross on it.'

'I have it.' She pulled the tin out and flipped it open. It was about the size of a cigar box and packed full with greaseproof paper packages and small metal cases.

'We're going to need one of those.' Drake pointed to one of three silver metal cylinders, like the ones used to hold expensive cigars, marked with a green dock leaf. 'But first, you're going to have to help me take my top off, I'm afraid.'

The struggle to get his broken arm out of several layers of clothing caused his vision to blur for a second, but finally, between the two of them they managed to get his arm free of its encumbrance.

He nodded his thanks to Tatiana. 'Well done. Alright, pop the top and pull the contents out carefully.'

Tatiana did as she was told, bringing out a tightly rolled tube of fabric.

'Good. There's a green flap on it, hold it by that and let it flop open. Make sure you don't touch the white parts, just the green ones.'

She did as he said, holding it up in front of her while gravity unrolled it for her. It stuck a couple of times and she had to give it a bit of a shake, but it was soon fully extended to a white cloth, about three inches wide and six long with two green "safe zones" at the ends.

Drake took a deep breath and nodded to her. 'Now lay it over the break lengthwise.'

She placed the cloth gently on his arm.

He gasped as even that slight pressure ignited sparks behind his eye, the agony almost unbearable, but then a tingling sensation spread up his arm as thousands of tiny needles loaded with a strong natural local anaesthetic pricked his skin and the pain faded to nothing. He counted to five, like he'd been told in basic training, then added an extra second for luck. 'That's enough, take it off.'

She placed the cloth to one side before touching his arm around the break experimentally. 'Can you feel this?'

He shook his head and grinned. 'Not a sausage.'

'Good.' She grunted in satisfaction. 'You might want to look away now.'

Drake nodded and turned his head to one side.

It was a strange sensation. He could feel the tugging on his skin, could feel the vibrations deep within his bones as she did whatever she was doing, but there was no pain at all, the anaesthetic extremely effective.

He heard her root around in the tin with the medical supplies again, then there was the sound of another canister opening and the smell of antiseptic as she wrapped saturated bandages around his arm.

'I need something to splint this. Have you got something I can use?'

Drake looked down at his arm. It was straight again and the wound was hidden underneath a thin layer of white cloth. 'There's a metal sheet under the lid of the med kit. It's designed to snap apart into six-inch lengths.'

She blinked at him in surprise then smiled in wonder, shaking her head. 'You British think of everything.'

Drake barked with laughter. 'I wish. If we did, then there wouldn't be any war and I'd be in a cafe somewhere instead of freezing my arse off in the woods.'

Tatiana laughed then opened the medical kit again. She quickly discovered the metal sheet and slid it out, then turned it over in her hands, finding the scored lines that allowed it to be broken cleanly. In only a few seconds she had two inch-wide strips, like ribs from a corset, which she bound tightly around his arm with twine provided for it in the kit and one of the straps from his knapsack detached to become a sling.

Tatiana gave the rest of his injuries a quick once over, painfully prodding his ribs underneath one of the more impressive bruises he'd earned tumbling from the remains of his aircraft, tutting and shushing him with a grin when he complained at the rough treatment. When she'd finished she got him dressed and settled comfortably, then sat facing him, extremely close in the confined quarters. 'There, all done.'

'Thank you.'

'You are welcome, Lieutenant.'

With the pain gone and his head clearer than it had been since the crash, Drake finally looked around. The two of them were underneath a tree, a pine or a spruce or something similar, in the small space, just enough to lie down in, between its lower branches and the ground. It was dry, almost warm, and fairly dark, most of the light and wind blocked by snow drifts on all side, which also effectively hid them from the outside world. Tatiana must have dragged him there while he'd been unconscious.

He smiled at her. 'And thank you for helping me. I hope I won't slow you down so much that you regret it.'

'If you do I'll leave you behind.'

The woman grinned, but Drake wasn't sure if she was entirely joking, neither was he sure if he wanted to know if she was or not. He pulled his knapsack towards him and turned his attention to the contents of the survival kit, laying it out on the ground between them.

Aside from the medical kit there was water and rations for three days, including chocolate, biscuits and a small bottle of brandy. There was also a small penknife, one of the Swiss-made ones that had useful tools that folded out, a length of fishing line, and some wire that was supposed to be for trapping rabbits and such. The penknife was the only thing he had that even approximated a weapon, although the inch-

and-a-half-long blade wasn't going to be much of a threat to anything, not even a rabid squirrel, and next to Tatiana's knives it was laughable. According to the RAC, the survival pack was enough to keep a pilot alive almost indefinitely if they were able to do at least a little hunting and find water, but he really didn't want to have to depend on the foraging skills he was supposed to have learnt during the survival training course all pilots went on, especially not in an unfamiliar forest in winter.

Tatiana saw what he was doing and added her own meagre supplies to his, but they were insignificant in comparison, just a couple of hip flasks and a few small packets of meat jerky which Drake suspected was reindeer. Fortunately she'd gotten a better haul from the soldiers. For a short-range patrol, the men had been carrying a surprising amount with them, as if they were scared of being trapped away from camp for some reason - perhaps a sign of their unfamiliarity with the terrain and weather. There was food, which unfortunately comprised mostly of the putrid dried sausage the Prussians favoured, but there was also enough schnapps for even a Muscovite to get rip-roaringly drunk.

Tatiana shook her head. 'The food will only last four days, perhaps five or six if we're careful. We will need to find more.'

Drake frowned at Tatiana. 'Why do we need that much? When it gets dark we can just sneak across the border. We'll be with Muscovite troops in a few hours.'

Tatiana rolled her eyes at him, once more making him feel stupid and naive. 'We can't get across the border here, there are too many Prussians.' She sighed and shook her head. 'Haven't you ever looked at the map in the Operations Room?'

Drake blinked. 'What map?' *For that matter, what Operations Room?*

'There is a big map on the wall in the Operations Room. It is kept updated with our intelligence on Prussian troop positions, much of which is provided by your own pilot, Charles Isaacs. How could you not have seen it?'

Drake shrugged and grinned cheekily. 'I don't really worry about what's on the ground; I have enough trying to teach Muscovite pilots how not to crash British aircraft.'

Tatiana stared at him coldly, long enough to make him think that he had gone too far, but then she chuckled. 'That's a fair point. You're a funny man, Lieutenant. I like you.' She slapped him on his good shoulder, jolting him and almost knocking him over. 'I'm hungry, what are we eating?'

Drake fished in his bag and brought out a pack of rations - a highly nutritious mixture of cereals, nuts and herbs, bound together with a hard, sugary, honey-like substance. It was designed to give the body everything it needed in one meal and by all reports it did. Unfortunately, it also tasted like a mixture of animal dungs held together by sewage and smelled just as bad. He'd lived off of them on a week-long training hike in the Brecon Beacons and had hoped to never have to eat another one in his life.

He tore the wrapping, then broke half off and gave it to Tatiana. 'Here. I apologise for the taste, but it's good for you, I promise, and we need to keep our energy up.'

Tatiana sniffed at the bar, doubtfully, then took a bite and started chewing. Her face lit up in delight. 'Mmm, thank you! It's good!' she said, speaking with her mouth open.

Drake stared at her for long seconds, looking for sarcasm in her expression, but found none and shrugged mentally. *What do you expect? These people eat beetroot with every meal.* He took a bite of his part of the bar, hoping that the powers that be had changed the recipe since he'd had one last and made it palatable, then grimaced when he found out that they hadn't. He chewed carefully, feeling the awful stuff tugging at his teeth and not particularly wanting to lose any.

After a few minutes he managed to loosen the mouthful up enough to swallow. 'By the way, you should call me Rudy; there's not much point on standing on ceremony any more, is there?'

Tatiana nodded and spoke around another mouthful of rations. 'Very well, Rudy, then you must call me Tanya; it is what my friends call me.'

Drake raised an eyebrow. 'What? We weren't friends before?'

She scoffed. 'Of course not! Before, you were just a strange man I had to rescue, but now we have shared food. In some parts of Russia that would mean we are married.'

She pointedly ignored his stare while she took another big bite of the rations, but then gave him another wide, and he had to admit extremely attractive, smile.

He laughed. 'And I thought all Russian humour revolved around vodka.'

'Not all. Most.'

Drake went to take another bite, but changed his mind and looked at the woman instead. 'So, if we can't go directly to the border, what do you suggest we do?'

'We go south.' Tanya answered with her mouth full, praying crumbs, but then finally realised what she was doing and covered her mouth with her hand. She chewed rapidly and swallowed before smiling sheepishly. 'Sorry. They tried to teach us table manners at officer training school, but most of us are from places where you eat meat straight from the fire with your hands.'

'Don't worry about it.' Drake smiled and waved away her apology; he had known boys with worse manners at Eton. 'You were saying?'

Tanya nodded. 'We have to go south. The charts in Operations were clear - the Prussians are strong all the way from here to the sea, but they thin out further south, nearer to the Baltic. We have to go around them.'

Drake nodded. 'Alright, so we go south a couple of days before we turn east. No problem.'

The woman shook her head. 'We have to go more than a hundred miles. That's at least four or five days if the weather stays good, but if it turns bad we might have to find somewhere to camp for a while. Which is why I said the food won't be enough.'

Drake frowned. 'We have to go that far south?'

'Yes, maybe further, depending on what we find.' She grinned. 'Don't worry; I was a guide before the war, I won't let us get lost. And besides, I have a map.'

Drake didn't return her smile, but just stared at the ground in silence, his mind racing. The ice was already closing in on Archangel and the latest estimates had said that the weather might turn too bad to fly or fight before the week was up. When that happened, Gwen, the Misfits and his fellow instructors would go back to England.

He shook his head. 'No. We have to get back before then; I need to be on the Arturo when it leaves, otherwise I'll be stranded in Muscovy.'

'I'm sorry, Rudy, but it's not possible. We can't get back any quicker than that. Not safely, anyway.' She smiled sympathetically and patted him on the knee. 'Perhaps we will be lucky and the weather will hold until we get back to Vaenga, but if not you can always winter with me - I have a nice dacha near Novosibirsk and it only gets a bit colder than this. Then, when the spring comes, you can go back to your friends.'

He smiled weakly. 'Thank you, that's jolly decent of you.'

They continued to eat in silence for a while, but eventually they finished and Drake started putting the supplies back into their bags. 'Right then, shall we go?'

'No, it's too easy for us to be seen during the day. We'll travel at night when the Prussians are asleep and looking only across the border.' She checked the chronograph on her wrist, an incredibly cheap-looking one with a scratched face - Muscovite standard issue. 'There's still a few hours until dark so we'll rest for now.'

She shifted over to sit next to him, her leg right up against his. She pulled one of her hip flasks from a pocket of her flightsuit, unscrewed the cap and offered it to him.

'Water?' Drake asked.

'Vodka.'

He shook his head. 'Thank you, but I shouldn't with the anaesthetic.'

'Da. That is probably for the best. And it leaves more for me!' She saluted him with the flask. 'To an easy walk home.'

Drake picked up the canteen from his survival pack and returned the gesture. 'To the walk home.'

As she swigged from the flask he took a long draught of the water and grimaced. 'Bleurgh, that tastes like it's been there for months.'

She winked. 'Why do you think we get supplied with vodka? It's much healthier.'

Drake laughed with her, but then the Muscovite turned serious. She took a big swig from the flask as if working up her courage for something, then looked him in the eye, her voice suddenly quiet. 'Do you know how the fight went, Rudy?' She blushed, ashamed. 'I was shot down in first pass, so I didn't see... Did we get any of them?'

'The fight went badly, I know at least three of the Wolfpack were shot down. I managed to bag one, though, before Gruber shot me down.'

'You got one?' Tanya smiled, her eyes lighting up. 'Then it was worth it!' She put her arm around him, pulled him close and kissed him on the cheek.

Drake struggled to free himself and she pulled back, frowning.

'What is wrong?'

'How can you say that? How was it worth it? It was a slaughter!'

She shook her head. 'Russia is a big country, there are millions of us. If one dies, ten more come. But the Barons... There are only a few of them. Killing one is worth four, five, perhaps even ten or twenty of us. Only losing three pilots is a miracle.'

It was Drake's turn to shake his head. 'The Barons aren't *that* good.'

She looked at him frankly. 'You've seen us fly - compared to us they are.'

'You...' He began to deny it, but found that he just couldn't; most of the pilots he'd trained in Muscovy had been mediocre at best. Compared to a Baron they weren't good. Compared to a Misfit, hell, even he was bad compared to a Misfit. He forced a smile, knowing that in some way her twisted logic made sense, but hating it nonetheless. 'You just haven't been given a chance to show how good you are. If you'd had even a week of training, then I'm sure you would think differently.'

'You are a bad liar, Rudy.' She laughed. 'I like you.'

She put the cap back on her hip flask, then patted him on the knee again. 'We should try to sleep.' She started to lie down, but then stopped and frowned at Drake's greatcoat. She reach out to finger the lapel and eyed it in disgust. 'What is this? Are you supposed to keep warm in this? It's... it's... I have no words.'

Drake laughed. 'I'm fairly sure the coat is supposed to be supplemented by a large dose of stiff upper lip and British stoicism, but you're right: I get the feeling that the RAC quartermasters had no idea how damn cold it was going to get here.'

'Take it off.'

Drake blinked at her as she started taking off her parka, not entirely sure what was going on.

She paused and glared at him when she saw he wasn't doing what she'd told him. 'Take it off!'

He gave her a half grin. 'Yes, ma'am!' He manoeuvred his arm out of the sling and awkwardly began to struggle out of his RAC greatcoat.

She took it from him and lay it on the ground, then pointed to it. 'Lie down.'

Tanya waited for him to get comfortable on his good side, then laid her parka over them. She then got under it and folded herself against his back.

He tried not to think about the woman pressed up against him and more especially what was poking him in the back, but it was impossible. 'Um, Tanya...'

'Do not get any ideas. This is how we survive the cold in Russia. Now shut up and sleep, I will wake you when it is time to go.'

'Alright, I'll try, but I'm not sure that I'll be able to.'

Whether it was the anaesthetic patch, the injury, or the bump on his head, in spite of his doubts, Drake found his eyes closing by themselves and almost immediately fell into darkness.

CHAPTER 4

Blood. There was so much blood everywhere. On the snow, the trees, the rocks. But this time it wasn't the cheerful Tanya holding knives and Prussians lying on the ground like so much meat; this time it was Hans Gruber from whose duelling sword the red liquid dripped and the bodies were his fellow instructors and the Misfits.

He searched the faces, grotesquely contorted with the agony of their death, but the one he dreaded finding wasn't there and he dared to hope.

'I'm sorry, but there's nobody waiting for you at Vaenga, Lieutenant Drake.' Hans Gruber's movie star smile widened as he stepped aside to reveal one final body draped hideously, bonelessly, over a rock behind him.

Drake fell to his knees in despair, but instead of giving up, the sight of Gwen's body provoked a rage in him that he couldn't contain.

He snarled as he surged back to his feet and leapt forwards, ready to exact his vengeance or at least join Gwen in death, but faceless Prussian pilots appeared, as if from nowhere, and grabbed him with clawed hands. He struggled against them, but it was no use and he was forced to watch impotently as Gruber picked up the body of the only woman he'd ever really loved and carried her away, deeper into the forest, laughing maniacally.

'No! No! NO!!! Bring her back!'

'Shut up!'

The dream faded only slowly as his brain became aware of the cold reality, but the last vestiges of the dream still clung and when he found that he couldn't move he fought, biting at the hand that covered his mouth and tearing at the arm holding him.

It was only when he realised that the swearing he was provoking was decidedly un-Prussian and female that he stopped struggling, but then, fully awake at last, he gasped as the full agony of his arm made its presence felt once more.

'For God's sake, Rudy, calm down!'

He tried to obey, but found that he couldn't; he was shivering violently. 'I can't. S-s-s-sorry.'

The warmth disappeared from his back as Tanya pulled away and a few seconds later there was a rapid clicking noise, followed by a blinding flare of light, which was accompanied by more swearing, before it dimmed to a mere glow.

He blinked, adjusting to the light of the small clockwork lantern they'd taken from the Prussians, and peered up into Tanya's concerned face.

'It's probably my arm.' He could barely get the words out through chattering teeth. 'The anaesthetic has worn off.'

She reached out to touch his brow, then his cheek. 'It's not just that. You're burning up.'

While she turned to look for one of the tubes he tried to get out of his flight suit, but his fingers wouldn't stop shaking and he couldn't get them to grasp the fasteners.

'Here, let me do that.'

In the end, all he could do was sit there and allow her to take care of him, as if he were a baby.

She applied the patch, then held the light over his arm to look at her handiwork. 'I don't like the look of the bruising, but I don't think there's any infection; there are no red veins or anything. I think the fever is just your body reacting to what it's going through.'

'Oh... Good.' He barely managed to squeeze out the words; even though the pain had receded with the application of the patch, his body was still shaking uncontrollably. 'Pills. In the tin. Willow bark. Two. P-p-please.'

The patches were only for local pain, for injuries and such, they did nothing for the rest of the body. For that, the med kit contained concentrated willow bark pills. They suppressed mild symptoms, like lowering a fever, helping a pilot stay healthy enough to continue avoiding capture, but they weren't particularly strong and did nothing to actually cure whatever was wrong. They were better than nothing, though.

After she had gotten him back into his clothing, Tanya fed him two pills, then held his water bottle for him when his hand shook too much to do so himself.

'Thank you.' Drake closed his eyes and waited for the pills to take effect. 'Is it dark yet?'

'The sun went down about half an hour ago, but it's still too early to get going.'

'Good; I think I'm going to need a while before I can walk.'

'Yes. You will.' The light went out and she settled back beside him under the parka, but didn't snuggle up to him.

They lay in silence for a while, as Drake's shaking subsided to an occasional shiver, the only noise the soft rustling of the needle-like leaves of the tree above them, but then Tanya's voice sounded in his ear. 'You were having a bad dream. You were calling out the name "Gwen"... Is that Gwen Stone? The Misfit? Are you her lover?'

'No, I'm really not. We grew up together and we're just friends.'

'But you wish she was more.'

'Of co...' Drake began to answer, but then stopped; for some reason he found that he no longer possessed the same certainty of only a few hours before. Perhaps it was the fever or perhaps his brush with death, but something had changed and he could no longer say that his desire for Gwen wasn't just what was left of his youthful infatuation. Even the gleam in her eye when she had said those fateful words to him no longer seemed the promise of a future, but rather regret at the necessity of a difficult conversation.

'I... um, well, I'm not sure actually. I love her as the sister I never had, but...' He tailed off in embarrassment; his persistent pursuit of Gwen and his subsequent proposal now seemed childish and not a little selfish.

'I understand.'

Tanya's voice was soft as she moved close again, her warmth seeping into him once more.

'It kills me that I won't know if anything happens to her over the next few days, though.' The vision of Gwen's broken corpse being carried away by Gruber sprang into his mind again and he gritted his teeth against the helplessness he'd felt, the helplessness he now felt. 'I know she can take care of herself; she's a Misfit, but with the Barons here and Baryshnikov acting so recklessly all bets are off.'

'She'll be fine. I'm sure of it. The Barons have gone up against the Misfits before and come off worse each time, I don't think this time will be any different. Do you?'

'No, I guess not.' Drake wasn't so callous as to tell her the truth, that every other time the Misfits had faced the Barons they'd had the entire RAC to keep the rest of the Fliegertruppe from them, not just a single Muscovite squadron with largely inexperienced pilots and an unreliable commander.

'So. If you are not Gwen Stone's man, whose are you?'

Drake chuckled at the Muscovite's turn of phrase. 'Apart from the King's, nobody's.'

'There is nobody waiting for you at home?'

'I have a couple of dogs.'

Tanya scowled, wrinkling her nose. 'You have dogs... Urgh, how did I know that you would?' She tutted and her hair brushed his neck as she shook her head. 'Such a man thing, cats are much better. And you know very well that I didn't mean that!' She slapped him none too gently on the thigh, dangerously close to his posterior. 'You have a girl waiting for you? Or a boy?'

He shook his head, laughing softly. 'No. Nobody'

'What about siblings?'

'None. I'm an only child.'

'I guess your parents will miss you.'

'I guess. You can never be too sure with my parents, though; I often got the feeling when I was growing up that they hadn't really wanted me, that I was just there to carry on the family name.'

'I don't know your parents, but I'm sure that's not true.'

Drake shrugged. 'Unfortunately, I think it's true of many of the children of the aristocracy in Britain; we have nannies and tutors taking care of us while we're growing up and then, as soon as we're old enough, we're packed off to boarding school. As a child I only really saw my parents for meals and even then I usually had half a dozen people or more between me and them.'

'You poor thing!'

There was silence for a moment, then Drake felt the parka being pulled up over his head. The sudden glow of the clockwork light made him blink and when he could see again, he found Tanya lying in front of him, a short stick holding the parka up over their heads like a tent. He hadn't felt her move.

'You said aristocracy? Does that mean you are a prince or something?'

'Not quite, just the son of an Earl.'

'Oh, is that all? So you are, what, Earl Rudy? Do I have to call you that now?'

Drake snorted. 'No! Until my father dies and I inherit his title I'm just Lord Rudyard Sebastian Augustus Cholmondeley Drake, Lord Drake for short.'

'Lord Rudyard Sebastian...' Tanya tailed off. 'I'm not sure I could remember all that even if I tried. I'll stick to Rudy, if you don't mind, my Lord.'

She gave him a mocking smile, bowing her head and Drake laughed again. 'I'd much prefer that, thank you.'

Tanya's smile faded and she turned serious. She grabbed the light and held it between them to illuminate him better and looked him up and down critically. 'How are you feeling?'

Drake realised that his arm no longer hurt and his trembling had completely stopped. He smiled. 'Much better, thank you.'

'Good, then I won't need to leave you behind.' She grinned, then took a bar of rations out of his bag and handed it to him. 'We'll go soon. Have some breakfast; you'll need your strength.'

An hour later, Tanya decided that the Prussians had had long enough to settle in for the night and start drinking and they set off into the freezing night, Drake following in the Muscovite's footsteps as she forged a path through the knee-deep snow. At first they went west, almost directly away from Muscovy, to get away from the highest concentration of Prussian forces, but then, after about five hours they turned south.

Drake was barely aware when they changed course. The most recent patch had begun to wear off after a couple of hours and the pain came back with a vengeance, along with the shivering. Tanya suggested using the last one, but he refused, wanting to keep it in case of a real emergency and instead just took a couple more pills. They weren't nearly enough, though, and he slipped into a kind of trance state where Tanya had to lead him by the hand and it was all he could do to stay on his feet and put one in front of the other. When they finally stopped, just before dawn, he was unconscious before his head hit the floor.

Two more nights passed like that. He had no idea how far they travelled; his memories were a nightmare of pain, while at the same time filled with a monotony that was broken only when Tanya dragged him into any available cover to avoid something he was too delirious to see. He had a vague impression of coming to a road cut through the forest and hunkering down in the trees to wait for a convoy of vehicles to go past, the vibrations in the ground almost indistinguishable from the tremors running through his body. He seemed to remember Tanya goggling at a pair of gigantic walkers in the long line of machines and excitedly commenting on them, but they made no impression on him and did nothing to bring him out of his stupor. He was also fairly sure they had crossed a river at some point, over a frozen narrows, with the ice creaking ominously at their weight.

Thankfully, though, when he collapsed every morning in whatever shelter Tanya could find them, the dream of Gwen's death didn't return.

While they were resting during the daylight hours of the fourth day, his fever finally broke and he opened his eyes to weak sunlight.

They were in a crude hut, which had seen far better days and obviously hadn't been used in quite some time. Cold light streamed in through numerous gaps in the walls, along with icy air, but it was better than being out in the open and the rotted floorboards provided good insulation from the frozen ground.

There was a familiar warmth against his back and he turned to find Tanya watching him. There were black circles under her eyes and he realised that, not only did she have the strain of shepherding him during the night marches, but she had probably not slept much during the days; this deep into enemy territory they needed to if not keep watch then remain alert while they rested, something she would have had to do for both of them while he'd been ill.

He smiled gratefully. 'You didn't leave me behind, then.'

'I was sorely tempted. More than once. But then I thought of how much of a reward your parents will give me for bringing you home to them.'

Drake chuckled. 'You've earned it. Thank you.'

She returned his smile. 'You're welcome, Rudy.'

From then on they moved a lot quicker and when they found a place to rest after two more nights of trudging through the unchanging Finnish forest Tanya announced that they were far enough south to risk crossing into Muscovy.

They started east from their latest shelter, a duck hunting blind on the shores of one of the dozens of iced over lakes, first thing in the morning. Drake had no idea how she knew where they were on her map, but she insisted that they were only half a dozen miles or so from the border which, that far south, no longer ran along a river, but through the wilderness. It was a walk of perhaps an hour or two, depending on the terrain, but it took much longer than that because Tanya brought them to a halt every few hundred yards and insisted that he wait while she scouted ahead.

The pauses took their toll on him, far more than the march itself, both mentally because he never knew whether Tanya would run into danger, but also physically because he ended up frozen stiff with the inactivity. The thought of how close he was to returning home kept him going, though; the weather had held out during the last few days and was still good for flying, meaning that the British expedition would almost definitely still be in Vaenga.

It was very slow going, but finally, in the small hours of the morning, when she reappeared there was a broad grin on her face instead of the serious look she usually had while they were moving.

'I've got something to show you, Rudy.'

Drake roused himself from under the fallen tree where he had taken cover and let her pull him to his feet, then staggered after her as best he could on stiff legs. It was pitch black and he was absolutely exhausted, so he didn't initially react when she stopped and it wasn't until she grabbed the collar of his greatcoat to give him a sharp tug that he stumbled to a halt.

'Come on, wakey wakey, Rudy! We're here!'

An extremely faint light blossomed in front of Drake, illuminating not only Tanya's face, but also a battered wooden signpost, sticking out of the frozen ground. He barely had time to register the fact that there was writing in Cyrillic burned into it before Tanya turned the light off again, but that brief glimpse was enough to send a surge of adrenaline through him which brought him full awake; they were in Muscovy, they were safe.

CHAPTER 5

Drake was almost knocked off his feet when Tanya threw herself at him, wrapping her arms around him and hugging him tightly.

'We're home, Rudy.'

There was a wetness on his cheek and he blinked in surprise when he realised that she was crying.

Hesitantly, he wrapped his good arm around her and held her back.

She pulled away after only a few seconds and her hand fumbled with his. 'Come on, there's an outpost a couple of miles away. We can be there by dawn and whoever's there will be able to call for some kind of vehicle to come pick us up. Maybe they'll even send a transport aircraft! We could be in Vaenga in time for lunch!'

The excitement in her voice was contagious and Drake couldn't help but laugh as she pulled him into motion, his tiredness and the cold completely forgotten in the face of the possibility of getting back to the airbase before the British expedition left.

The sky was lightening by the time Tanya dragged Drake into a crouch within a copse of trees.

'There it is.'

'Where?' Drake looked to where she was pointing, but couldn't see anything through the morning mist.

'Fifty yards ahead. Between the two big firs.'

Drake squinted, scanning the area. 'All I can see are a few bushes and a mound of earth...'

Tanya rolled her eyes. 'It *is* the mound, dummy! Under that is a reinforced concrete bunker with a dedicated telegraph line connected to a central exchange in St. Petersburg and mounted machine guns covering all approaches. There are thousands of bunkers, just like this one, every few miles along our entire western border. During peacetime they're only manned by local volunteers who are provided with food and a stipend, but since we entered the war they each have at least four soldiers assigned to them, but the ones closer to the combat areas have entire companies.'

'So there should be soldiers in there.'

'Yes. And at least one of them should be awake and looking out for the enemy, which is why we've stopped here.' She grinned. 'I don't want to be shot by my own side after all we've gone through.'

'That would be a little bit annoying.' Drake chuckled, nodding earnestly. 'So, how do we avoid that?'

'Like this.' Tanya lit the clockwork lantern, holding it against her chest so that it could only be seen from in front of her. She moved it up and down deliberately three times, then extinguished it again.

'Now what?'

The words were hardly out of his mouth before an answering light came on in the mound, almost invisible in the morning haze. It moved from side to side three times, then winked out.

Tanya smirked at him. 'Now *that.*'

She grabbed his hand and together they jogged across the open ground, giving Drake his first good look at the bunker.

The mound of earth atop the military installation was about five feet high and five yards wide atop a slight rise. It was planted with bushes to better camouflage it, although they had obviously been kept fairly trimmed so as not to obstruct the view slit, which went all the way around the bunker just above ground level, giving it a commanding view of the surrounding area.

Tanya took them to the far side where there was a ramp down into the ground concealed beneath more bushes and Drake followed her down. It was steep and damp, open as it was to the elements, but a metal grid on the floor kept it from being dangerously slippery. A heavy-looking door was standing invitingly open for them at the base of the ramp and a man, bundled up in a Muscovite parka with his hood pulled low against the cold, was waiting for them in the doorway. As they got nearer, Tanya began babbling to him in Russian and the man smiled, nodding, and gestured for them to go inside.

The bunker was far larger than Drake had been expecting. It was an open space, about three yards high, empty, apart from a narrow walkway going around the wall, which provided a platform from which to look out of the observation slit, and a circular hole in the floor, through which was coming a soft glow, illuminating an ornate brass spiral staircase.

He wandered over to the staircase and ran his hand over the intricate handrail, tracing the ubiquitous cogs, interwoven with military devices such as projectiles, swords and guns to form a tubular lacework. It traced a circle around the hole, serving as a safety rail, before spiralling elegantly down around thin wrought iron stairs composed of extremely realistic overlapping leaves. As he bent to take in the details more closely, he wondered why such an artwork had been created for such a remote place and whether there was one in all of the bunkers Tanya had mentioned.

He was so fascinated by the staircase that he hadn't noticed the blood on the back of the parka of the man who'd let them in, nor did he see the two other men, dressed in snow gear that was definitely not Muscovite, who appeared from the deep shadows on either side of the door.

Tanya did, though, and she spun in place, her knives appearing in her hands as if from nowhere. However, before she could do more than lunge in the direction of one of the men, the first man struck her in the head with his rifle butt and she collapsed to the floor like a sack of spuds.

'Tanya!'

Drake heard the commotion behind him and spun. He began to leap to the woman's defence, but the rifles of all three men swung towards him and he immediately thought better of it.

The man who'd opened the door for the looked Drake up and down. 'You are British are you not? A Misfit?' The man's English was precise with only a hint of an accent, betraying at least a few years of education in England. He was most likely an officer.

Drake drew himself up. 'Aviator Lieutenant Drake, Royal Aviator Corps. Serial number...'

The officer waved for him to stop. 'I don't recognise your name so you are not a Misfit.' He said something to his companions in a language that Drake didn't recognise and they lowered their rifles then bent to pick up Tanya's knives from the floor where they had fallen before searching her.

The officer watched them for a moment, then turned back to Drake. 'Will you be a gentleman and hand over your weapons, swearing to me that they are all you have, or do I have to order my men to search you?'

Drake nodded. 'I will surrender my weapons.'

'Good choice.'

Drake fished around in his knapsack, brought out the penknife and handed it over with a grin.

The officer blinked and turned it over in his hands, pulling out the blade and the other implements in turn, before looking up at Drake again. 'This is truly the only weapon you have?'

'On my honour as a gentleman.'

The man looked at him sceptically, but nonetheless nodded his acceptance. He put the penknife in his pocket, then gestured at the staircase. 'Would you go downstairs, please, Aviator Lieutenant Drake?'

'Of course.' Drake started to go, then turned back as something occurred to him. 'Please tell me you have tea down there; I'm gasping.'

Instead of answering, the man just gave Drake a cold look, then turned away and spoke to his men again. They picked up Tanya between them and, while one of them climbed up to the walkway, the other put her over his shoulder. When Drake saw her limp and too still form he feared the worst, but as the guard carried her past he was relieved to see her chest rising and falling.

The opulence of the staircase continued in the living quarters below. There was wood panelling on the walls, thick rugs on the floor, a couple of sofas, a full bookcase, and a wooden table laid with a cooked breakfast, which was still steaming. A moderately-sized clockwork electrical heater, wound by means of what looked like the pedals and chain from a penny-farthing, stood against the wall to one side, providing warmth and presumably hot water without any smoke to give away the position of the bunker. Soft electric sconces provided illumination and there were large landscape paintings providing views of the surrounding countryside in spring and summer on all four walls, as if to compensate for the lack of windows.

Although there was no escaping the fact that it was underground, it had more the aspect of a cabin in the woods than a fortification and it was extremely impressive for a hole in the ground in the middle of the forest.

The soldier lay Tanya down on one of the sofas, then disappeared down one of the two dark corridors leading off the room, leaving Drake alone with the officer, who wandered over to warm his hands on the heater. He pulled back the hood of the bloody Muscovite parka to reveal shockingly blonde hair, then turned to warm his back while he regarded Drake with a pair of the brightest blue eyes that he had ever seen.

'You are a long way from home, Lieutenant.'

'Yes, but unlike you *I* was invited to Muscovy.'

The man smiled coldly and nodded, conceding the point. 'Well, *unlike you*, I will see my home again soon.' He gestured towards the table. 'Please, make yourself comfortable. Help yourself to food and drink.'

'I'd rather see to my friend first.'

The man shrugged. 'Suit yourself.'

Drake knelt down next to Tanya and gently turned her head to look at where she had been hit. There was a large lump and her hair was matted with blood, but there was no sign of a fracture or anything when he gently explored it and she moaned in pain at his touch, which was encouraging.

The soldier came back into the room and said something in the unfamiliar language, which Drake now assumed was Finnish. The officer said a few words in reply then walked over to Drake. 'Someone will be here to get you shortly, I suggest you have some food while you can; it is a long drive and I cannot guarantee that you will be kept in such luxurious conditions where you are going.'

'And where is that?'

'You are being moved to the nearest Prussian army camp. They are better equipped to hold you than we are.'

'You could always let us go, then nobody has to worry about us.'

'Ah, the British sense of humour in the face of insurmountable odds.' The man smiled grimly, with no humour of his own. 'Try to hold on to it; you will need it.'

Before Drake could reply, he turned away and climbed back up the stairs, leaving the soldier to keep an eye on them.

'Rudy?'

Tanya's voice was soft, but strong and when she looked up at him there was no sign of concussion, something that years of rugby at Eton had taught him to recognise. He knelt next to her again. 'How are you feeling?'

She continued speaking in a low voice that he could barely hear. 'I'm fine; they didn't actually knock me out - I knew I couldn't win so I let them think they did.'

Drake stared at her. 'You let them... You...' He trailed off.

She smiled at his expression. 'I trained as a prizefighter before the war so I know how to roll with a punch, but never mind that now. If we're going to get away we need to go now, before whoever is coming arrives; they'll be watching us too closely when we're being moved.'

The Finnish soldier was behind Drake and he couldn't see him, but he could almost feel the barrel of the rifle pointed at his back. He shook his head. 'We can't. Even if we could get past this one, we'd never get up the stairs without being shot by the other two.'

Tanya's face turned cold, the smile disappearing in an instant. 'Yes, we *might* be killed, but if we do nothing, we will most likely spend the rest of the war rotting in a Prussian prison camp. I for one would rather take the chance.'

Drake found the change in Tanya's expression frightening, but he couldn't help but agree with the sentiment. He gave her a curt nod. 'Very well, what can I do?'

'Our only hope is to take care of the man down here without alerting the other two. I just need you to distract him distracted, then I'll take care of the rest. Go ask if you can use the bathroom and make sure you're between him and me.'

Drake had no idea how she was going to pull off the attack on the man silently, but there was no uncertainty in Tanya's eyes, just a fierce determination, so he nodded and decided to give her the benefit of the doubt. 'Good luck.'

'You too.' He shifted his weight to stand up, but before he could, she reached out to grab him by the front of his greatcoat and pulled him into a kiss.

Drake was taken so completely by surprise that he barely had a chance to register that their lips were touching before she was pulling back.

'What are you...? Why did...?'

'There you go asking multiple questions at the same time again.' She grinned. 'I'll answer them later, but for now, just shut up and concentrate on not getting yourself killed.'

Drake had always had the gift of the gab, but for some reason, he kept finding himself lost for words around the woman and all he could do was nod.

He stood and brushed his knees off, even though the carpet was cleaner than his clothes, then wandered towards the soldier, trying to look as nonchalant as possible.

'Um, hello.'

The man didn't say anything, but the way the barrel of his rifle shifted slightly upwards was eloquent enough and Drake stumbled to a halt a couple of paces from him.

He ran his hand nervously through his filthy hair. 'I was, uh, wondering if I could, um, go to the bathroom?'

The man jerked his gun towards one of the corridors and that was all the opening Tanya needed. She flowed past Drake and in less than a second, as if by magic, the man was on the floor, choking for breath and his rifle was in her hands.

Drake gaped at her. 'How...?'

She rolled her eyes and motioned for him to be quiet and stay where he was, then made her way to the staircase and peered up.

Drake followed her, but she put her hand on his chest and glared at him, then stabbed a finger at the floor, leaving him in no doubt that she intended to take care of the other two men on her own.

He didn't like it, but he had seen what she could do and knew he would just get in her way, so he nodded his acquiescence and backed off a couple of steps.

She nodded in return, slipped off her boots, then went up the staircase silently and disappeared from sight.

After a couple of seconds of silence all hell broke loose, the sound of screams and gunfire deafening in the enclosed space.

Since there was no longer any need for stealth, Drake raced up the stairs. He had no idea what he could possibly do to help, but he didn't care; he wanted to be on hand just in case.

The shooting stopped before he was half-way up and as he rounded the last bend of the staircase he came face to face with the other soldier.

He cried out and swerved to the side, trying to avoid the bullets he knew were coming, but tripped on the last step and fell, tumbling to the bare concrete floor of the bunker. He kept moving, though, and rolled back onto his feet with his good fist raised, ready to defend himself to the last.

'Rudy? What are you doing?'

Slowly, it dawned on Drake that the man he'd been so frightened of was just lying on the safety rail, his body broken and limp, blood dripping from multiple bullet wounds. He straightened from the fighting crouch his boxing instructor had taught him and turned to find Tanya leaning against the wall, watching him with a broad grin on her feet, the other man, the officer, lying inert at her feet.

'Um... Helping?' Drake chuckled nervously, even as he stared at the officer; his head was twisted around further than should have been possible and his blue eyes were looking right at him.

Tanya laughed, but then scowled suddenly. 'Well, if you wanted to help, you should at least have brought my shoes up with you.' She tutted and shook her head in exasperation. 'Come on, let's go get our things. We have to get out of here.'

They raced back downstairs and Drake grabbed his bag while she went down one of the corridors to the kitchen to find food. After some consideration, he also picked up the bloody Muscovite parka that the man had discarded and put it on over his greatcoat; he was fed up of stuffing leaves inside his flightsuit in an effort to keep warm.

Tanya came back out and saw him. She nodded in approval, but said nothing as she led the rush back upstairs and through the door into the dank tunnel.

They raced up into the cold daylight and immediately came up short when they saw what was waiting for them.

The soldiers that had been sent to get them had obviously heard the firing; they had set up a heavy machine gun to cover the exit of the ramp and placed a couple of men on top of the bunker behind them to cut off any possible retreat.

Tanya grinned at Drake as she put up her hands. 'Oh well, at least I got to kill a few more invaders.'

This time she didn't see the rifle butt coming and neither did Drake.

CHAPTER 6

When Drake opened his eyes he found himself face down in the back of a steam wagon, his cheek pressed against the freezing cold and rusting iron floor. A ringing in his ears and the dull thump of a headache to beat all headaches almost blocked out the sound of the engine, but they were merely a discomfort compared to the sharp agony in his arm, which was doubled underneath him. The continuous shaking of the inadequately-sprung wagon as it trundled along were fiery pinpricks in the broken bone, but occasionally there was a larger jolt as the wagon made its way over rough ground which shot a flare of agony up his arm and set stars flaring in his vision. He groaned and tried to roll off the arm, but his back came up against something hard which prevented him from doing so and he looked up into the face of a Finnish soldier, who grinned evilly then drew back the boot he'd bumped into and kicked him in the kidneys. He gasped, writhing at the fresh pain and rolled back the other way, but immediately came up against another obstacle - Tanya. She was on her back, still unconscious, her left cheek covered with blood and her lip and eye on that side black and swollen.

His pain was all but forgotten at the sight of her and he struggled to sit up.

'Tanya!'

He reached out to shake her gently by the shoulder and she moaned. Her eyes flickered open, but they didn't focus on him and after a few seconds they fluttered closed again. It had been long enough for him to see that her pupils were uneven, though.

'Wake up, Tanya, come on.' Drake shook her a bit rougher, knowing that she shouldn't sleep if she had a concussion.

She moaned again, louder this time and her eyes opened again. She looked up at him, but he could see that it was a struggle for her to focus on him. 'Rudy. We're alive, then.'

Drake smiled weakly. 'For now at least. Come on, let's get up; the floor is too cold, we can't stay here.'

None of the four white-clad soldiers sitting in the corners of the canvas-covered passenger compartment lifted a finger as he struggled to half-help, half-lift her from the floor, they just laughed among themselves every time the wagon lurched or bumped and they fell. Eventually he got her onto one of the wooden benches running along the walls and flopped down next to her.

While the exertion had exhausted him and he had to wait for a sudden bout of dizziness to pass, it seemed to have done her a bit of good and she was much more aware of what was going on around her.

'Well, I had fun in the bunker, let's do it again sometime.'

She gave him a meaningful look, tilting her head minutely at the soldiers and Drake couldn't help but groan. 'I don't think either of us are in any shape for more excitement and besides, I have no idea what you actually were before the war, but I've only ever been a pilot - I don't do guns and knives and hand to hand fighting, I do Harridans and Spitsteams.'

'Why, whatever do you mean, Rudy? I'm *only* a pilot too.' She smiled slyly. 'You're probably right, we should rest for a few minutes before making our escape.' She put her arm on his hand. 'You shouldn't sell yourself so short, though; I saw the way you leapt up those stairs.'

'Yes. And fell on my face.'

'Well, it's the thought that counts and we'll work on your fighting skills for next time.' She grinned widely at him, revealing a couple of missing teeth and reddened gums in a bloody mouth.

He frowned. 'How are you feeling? It looks like they knocked you around pretty badly.'

She chuckled, then winced, putting her hand to her jaw and wiggling it experimentally. 'I guess they recognised the main threat when they saw it.' She shrugged. 'I'll survive. I've had worse. What about you?'

'I feel like I've been pulling high G's for a few hours and then boxed eight rounds with the heavyweight champion of the Kingdom. With a broken arm.'

'Only eight rounds? Then you have a few left in you!'

She smiled again then put her hand to her head and swayed, pantomiming feeling faint. It wasn't a very convincing performance and Drake wondered what she was doing until she used the excuse to lean against him, putting her mouth close to his ear.

'I recovered my knives at the bunker and they didn't find them. If we bide our time the guards will probably get bored, maybe doze off, and we'll take our chances then.'

'Why are you so determined to escape? Our luck is going to run out at some point.'

She lifted her head slightly to peer up into his eyes, so close that Drake could almost feel her lips on his again. 'Have you not heard about their prison camps? About the inhumane conditions in them?'

'No.' Drake's mouth went dry and he shook his head. 'Should I have?'

'Quite a few soldiers have managed to escape the camps with the help of underground networks in the occupied countries. According to them, they and other inmates are often forced to work themselves to death, mining or cutting trees or such. My government informed your War Ministry about the camps months ago, I would have thought they'd have told you.'

Again, Drake shook his head. 'We know the Prussians have to have somewhere to keep prisoners of war, just like we do, but we haven't been told what their camps are like.' He paused, looking around at the soldiers. None of them were showing any signs of inattention, although it was still early in the journey. 'If people have escaped, then maybe we can do the same. We don't have to try now when we have four guards and we're both weak.'

It was Tanya's turn to shake her head. 'I doubt we will be able to; there was not a single pilot among the soldiers who have escaped.'

'No pilots? Well, that's not too surprising, given the number of soldiers who must've been captured and the number of pilots.'

'No, you don't understand. I'm not only saying that no pilot has escaped, I'm saying that the soldiers who make it out report not having seen a *single* pilot in the camps. *All* the pilots go elsewhere and never come back.' She gave him a meaningful look. 'Or maybe they don't go anywhere at all...'

Despite Tanya's melodramatic turn of phrase and presentation of the facts, a shiver ran through Drake and it had nothing to do with the cold in the back of the wagon. The implications were horrifying, but in some way they made sense; for the first time ever in a war, air power had taken on more of an importance than ever before. Battles were now being won and lost by air support, traditional fortifications had been rendered almost useless, and cities were not being sacked by armies but flattened by bombers. The elite warriors were no longer those who could swing a sword best or shoot the fastest or most accurately, but rather the pilots controlling the skies. *They* were now the most valuable commodity in the war and it was therefore in the interest of both sides that any captured pilots were never allowed to return to the fight.

'We're still alive, so they can't be just killing every pilot they capture out of hand.'

'These guys are Finnish. Maybe they haven't gotten the message yet.'

'Or maybe the local Prussian commander has to make the decision or something. Whatever the reason, there's no way I can hide the fact that I'm a pilot, but you could still say you're just a soldier.'

'I didn't abandon you to die in the forest and I'm not going to do so now. We're in this together. We'll just wait our chance, as I said.'

'Alright.' Drake nodded.

'Good. Now get some rest; we'll need it.'

Tanya snuggled further into his side and in moments was snoring gently through her blood-blocked nose.

Drake looked down at her in surprise and not a little envy; he had no idea how she could possibly sleep under the circumstances, but then one of her eyes opened just a slit and looked up at him and he realised that again she was play-acting.

Drake gave her an almost imperceptible nod, then closed his eyes, following her lead; if the soldiers thought they were asleep they would be more likely to relax their guard.

The trouble was that he was finding it almost impossible to just *act* like he was sleeping; the combination of the fact they had walked all night and the warmth of the Muscovite parka, so much better suited to the weather than his greatcoat, meant that he kept dozing off for real. He drifted in and out of consciousness, jerking awake every so often as the wagon bumped along. He looked around with bleary eyes each time, but the guards never seemed to take their gaze off the two of them, most likely having seen what remained of the men in the bunker. The view through the open back of the wagon remained unchanged as well, just seemingly endless forest and an ever-receding dirt road that was not much more than a track between the trees.

At some point he must have dropped off completely because it was near midday when he felt Tanya's hand squeeze his thigh. He was instantly awake, but this time he managed to keep his eyes shut and feign sleep.

'Be ready.'

Her whispered words in his ear sent adrenaline surging through his body and it was all he could do not to twitch and give the game away. As it was, he couldn't stop himself opening his eyes a crack to see what was going on.

He didn't like what he saw - only two of the guards were asleep, their rifles limp on their laps, but the other two were still alert.

'No.'

His reply was just a breath, but he knew she'd heard him because she stiffened and growled. 'Yes. Now or never.'

He sighed. 'Alright.'

'I'm right, you're left.'

Drake swivelled his eyes to look at the man on his left, sitting next to the tailboard of the wagon. Of the two awake guards he was perhaps the least threatening; he looked young, probably still in his teens, and his attention kept drifting to the passing scenery.

'On three.'

Drake glanced down at Tanya and found her gazing up at him. She fixed him with her blue eyes, so determined and resolute and he found his doubts and fears receding slightly.

'One.'

He took a deep breath, feeling Tanya's hand on his arm squeezing him, giving him strength. He visualised what he had to do - the three steps to the young soldier, the punch to his jaw, then the grab for the gun which he would use to club the other guard.

'Two.'

He tensed his muscles and clenched his fist, physically preparing himself for the violence to come.

Tanya's mouth opened to give the word and he felt her body tense against his, but before she could say it, the wagon screeched to a halt and the opportunity to escape was lost as all four guards came instantly alert.

One of the soldiers at the front of the wagon shouted a question, which was answered by someone in the driver's cab. Drake could understand neither, but the meaning was made perfectly clear when the wagon once more lurched into motion, swerving hard to the right as it did so.

Suddenly, the picturesque but monotonous view of empty forest that they'd had for hours through the gap at the rear of the wagon was replaced by a far more sinister one of grey Prussian vehicles in a line that stretched off into the distance.

Tanya stared at the sight, then sighed and sat up. She slumped on the bench and wrapped her arms disconsolately around herself. 'Well, that's that. No use pretending to sleep anymore.'

Drake smiled wryly. 'We could always actually sleep, that way we'll at least be a bit rested for whatever's coming.'

Tanya grinned. 'Good idea and that gives me an excuse to snuggle up with you again.'

It was dark by the time the wagon finally stopped.

They were shaken unceremoniously awake, then hustled out of the vehicle and handed over to a couple of Prussian soldiers with serious faces and efficient-looking machine guns. They barely had time to register the fact that they were on some kind of military installation before being shoved up a couple of steps and through the door of a brick building.

An officer in a smart grey uniform was waiting for them inside. He was short and weaselly, with slicked-back black hair and small round glasses and was carrying a clipboard. He would have been at home in any clerk's office in the world, but instead he was standing within what looked like a sports changing room, with wooden benches against three walls and pegs above them for hanging clothes.

The man looked them up and down, taking note of Tanya's uniform before pulling aside Drake's Muscovite parka to peer at the rank insignia on his greatcoat. He nodded in satisfaction. 'Name, please, Aviator Lieutenant?'

Drake gave him a smile. 'Lord Rudyard Sebastian Augustus Cholmondeley Drake, but you may call me, "my Lord".'

The man returned the smile, but it was cold and snakelike, had nothing of humour in it and lasted for less than a second. He looked down and scribbled on the sheet of paper attached to the clipboard, then turned his attention to Tanya. 'And you, Praporshik?'

'Tatiana Guseva.'

He made another note, then pointed to the bench at the back of the room. 'Go there and strip, please. Take everything off.'

Drake glanced at Tanya and opened his mouth to protest, but she just shook her head and walked to the back of the room where she began undressing.

Drake gave the man a glare, receiving an impassive stare in reply, then went to join her.

When she saw him struggling with his arm, she stopped what she was doing and moved to help him.

She was down to just her extremely unflattering thermal underwear and Drake flushed, embarrassed and made a point of looking only at her face.

She saw his expression and smiled. 'Show no weakness.'

She finished helping him out of his many layers, then stepped away and quickly took off the rest of her clothes, then turned to face the three men. She held her head up, not showing any emotion and making no effort to cover herself.

Drake removed his undershorts rather more hesitantly, then took a deep breath and turned to face the men, holding his broken arm tightly to his chest. He ground his teeth together when he saw the two guards leering openly at Tanya, but held his tongue and tried to emulate the Muscovite woman's dignity. He couldn't, though; he'd never liked being naked, even in the shower after games at Eton, it had always made him feel vulnerable. It also didn't help that he was all too aware of how cold it was and the effect that had on him. Thankfully, at least for him, the guards were too busy staring at Tanya to make any jokes at his expense.

The clerk stepped forwards and inspected Drake clinically. 'Your arm is broken, yes?'

Drake nodded.

He looked at the soiled bandages and frowned. 'It has been taken care of?'

'By Praporshik Guseva, yes.'

The man grunted disparagingly. 'We will have a proper doctor look at it. Turn around.'

Drake turned to face the wall, feeling the man's eyes roaming up and down him, searching for other injuries.

'Good.'

Drake turned back around as the man moved to stand in front of Tanya. The two guards craned their necks to look around the clerk when he blocked their view and Drake winced when his fists clenched involuntarily, sending a shock of pain up his arm.

The man looked at Tanya's face. 'Open your mouth.'

She did as she was told, displaying her missing teeth, and he grunted again before making a note. He stepped back and looked her up and down. There was nothing remotely sexual or interested in the way he did so, though, and Drake was grateful for that.

'Turn.'

Tanya turned in place and caught Drake looking at her. She gave him a quick wink before staring at the wall.

'Good.'

The man pointed to a pile of clothes at the side of the room. 'Leave your things here and put those on.'

Drake immediately scurried over to the clothes. They turned out to be very basic underwear, some gym shoes and a jumpsuit, not unlike his flightsuit, but in red. Tanya followed him more slowly, to all appearances unconcerned about her nakedness, and began dressing unhurriedly.

They watched as the clerk began rummaging through their uniforms, pulling things out of pockets and emptying the survival pack, which the Finnish soldiers had brought with them.

He found Tanya's knives in their concealed sheathes in her parka and gave her an inquisitive look.

She shrugged. 'There are bears in these woods.'

The knives went in a pile, along with the discarded flightsuits, underwear and Drake's bloody parka, but he put some of their belongings back in the survival pack, including what little food, water and medical supplies remained. He found Drake's penknife, which Tanya had recovered for him, opened it, snorted, then put it in the pack as well, before walking over to them.

'Take these.' He gave Tanya her parka and the knapsack and Drake his greatcoat. 'Put them on and follow me.'

Tanya helped Drake into his greatcoat, then the two of them followed the clerk out of the door and back out into the night.

They rounded the corner of the building and Drake stumbled to a halt in shock as the rest of the facility was finally revealed.

The guard following him roughly pushed him back into motion, but he continued to gape at the sight.

There were half a dozen more brick buildings next to the one they had come out of and other, more military-looking ones of various sizes beyond them, but it was the four huge floodlit hangars and the MU9's and MU10's half-hidden within them, a few hundred yards away across a large airfield, which were all he really saw - they had been brought to an airbase. He tried to slow down to get a better look at the aircraft, but a prod in the back kept him going and before he had taken more than a few steps, he was herded towards one of the newer military buildings. The exterior door led directly into a large room, which was filled with soldiers wearing grey uniforms similar to the clerk's, working at desks, quietly performing administrative tasks. To a man, they looked up and went still as the two prisoners were brought in, but the clerk didn't spare them a glance and just marched straight to a partitioning wall at the back of the room and knocked on a closed door.

'Come!'

At the call from within, the clerk opened the door and smartly marched in, clicking his heels together as he came to a halt in front of a large wooden desk. As the guards shoved Drake and Tanya into position behind him, he bowed crisply, then straightened and stared at the wall in front of him, waiting to be noticed. The man behind the desk didn't look up or acknowledge him in any way, though, he just continued writing in a small black book, which looked very like a flight log to Drake - he had a very similar one himself.

Drake gave the man a cursory glance, but when he didn't bother to even acknowledge them he ignored him disdainfully and instead gazed around the room. It was almost as large as the one they had come through, taking up the entire width of the building and had windows on either side, through which the rest of the air base could be seen, although unfortunately the aircraft weren't in view from where Drake was standing.

As for the office itself, there were the obligatory row of file cabinets behind the desk with maps of the local area pinned above them and the wall to one side was covered with grainy photographs of aircraft. There was no sign whatsoever of any personal effects of the man who occupied it, though, which Drake thought was strange; in his experience it didn't matter how temporary an office or ready room were, the people who used them always found some way to make it their own.

Drake's attention was drawn back to the desk as the man capped his fountain pen and laid it to one side, then sat back in his chair, finally lifting his head to look at them.

Which was when Drake got his biggest surprise of the evening; it was the man who had shot him down almost a week ago - Hans Gruber, leader of the Crimson Barons and erstwhile Hollywoodland movie star.

Drake had only ever seen the man in black and white motion pictures and newsreel, or on crudely coloured posters, so it was no wonder he hadn't recognised him, especially seeing as the hair that was always pictured as being so blonde was in fact a dirty light brown. It was also receding quite sharply at the temples and he thought he'd detected a developing bald spot when he'd been looking down, although the man kept it quite long in an attempt to hide the fact.

Drake was barely able to contain a smirk; no wonder the man wore a flight helmet as much as he could in his films and was always seen with a hat whenever he was out and about.

'What have we here?' Gruber asked in German.

In response to the question the clerk finally moved, snapping his clipboard smartly up in front of him as if it were a parade manoeuvre.

'Praporshik Tatiana Guseva and Lord Aviator Lieutenant Rudyard uh... Drake.'

Drake had to hide another smirk as the man mixed up the order in which his titles should come, then didn't bother giving his full name.

'Drake?' Gruber showed real interest for the first time when he heard the name. He looked at Drake and spoke in English with a heavy American accent. 'Of the Oxfordshire Drakes?'

When Drake nodded in acknowledgement, Gruber surged to his feet and came out from behind the desk to stand in front of him, completely ignoring Tanya. He frowned when he saw the arm that Drake was holding against his chest and turned to the clerk, reverting to German. 'Has his injury been seen to?'

'Not yet, sir.'

'Make sure it's taken care of as soon as I finish with him.'

'Yes, sir.'

Gruber turned back to Drake and the stern expression left his face, replaced by the wide smile that had made him so famous and had caused so many women, and not a few men, to throw themselves at his feet. Drake was amused to see that the smile, like his hair, was also deeply flawed, with many of the molars capped by a silvery metal. He also caught a distinct whiff of halitosis when he switched back to English.

'Lord Drake, it is an honour to meet you. I would offer you my hand, but it seems both of yours are busy. Don't worry, we will get that seen to soon.'

'Thank you.'

'I only recall shooting down one British aircraft recently, so I assume you are the man in the Harridan who killed one of my pilots?'

Drake nodded. 'I am.'

'I must admit I am surprised you survived, let alone with so few injuries.'

Drake shrugged. 'I have superior British engineering to thank for that.'

'Ah yes,' Gruber nodded sagely. 'The famous Gwenevere Hawking protective cage. It is a shame it has only saved you for captivity. We will speak again, after you have eaten and rested.'

Gruber turned away before Drake could reply and one of the guards immediately grabbed him and pulled him from the room.

CHAPTER 7

They were marched from the administration building directly to a medical centre, only two buildings down. It was filled with clean-sheeted beds in two long neat rows and fully-equipped with all sorts of electrical machines and mechanical marvels, most of which were switched off and silent and none of which Drake recognised.

He was sat on a bed while a doctor, assisted by a male nurse, took the splints off his arm then unwrapped the dirty and over-used bandages. When he gasped and squirmed at the fresh agony, clutching at the sheets with his free hand, the doctor injected something into the arm, half above and half below the break. The pain almost immediately went away, but Drake swayed, blinking and gasping for breath as his senses dulled and a humming began in his ears, like a swarm of bees.

The last thing he remembered before the darkness overwhelmed him was Tanya leaping off the bed next to his, calling his name.

Drake woke with the first light of dawn streaming through bar-covered windows. He was in a tiny room with bare brick walls, a metal door, a tin bucket in the corner and just enough room for two beds. Tanya was lying on the other bed, her hand outstretched towards him and he reached out to her, but stopped short, amazed, when he realised that, while his arm itched like hell, it didn't hurt in the slightest. In fact, for the first time since the crash he was feeling rested and like his normal self. He sat up and gingerly pulled up his sleeve to look at his injury and found some kind of waxy wrapper where the break was. He poked at it experimentally, wondering how he was going to scratch the itch.

'Don't you dare pick at it.' His movement had woken the Muscovite woman and she lifted her head to smile at him, her eyes bleary with lack of sleep.

'What happened to me?'

'The doctors said you had a bad reaction to the drug they gave you. Something about it reacting with the willow pills. They forgot to ask you if you'd been taking anything and you almost died apparently.'

She said it so matter-of-factly that Drake just had to laugh. 'Well that's alright then.' He flexed his hand, testing the muscles in his arm gently. 'This is incredible! What on earth did they do? Give me a new one or something?' He said it jokingly, but was fully prepared to accept it if she said yes; it was unbelievable that his arm was as good as new and he wouldn't be surprised if it was one of the clockwork ones the Japanese were reported to have developed.

Tanya shrugged and waved a hand vaguely. 'They used a few machines, shot some electrics into your arm and said something about knitting bones that I didn't understand. They also said that it wasn't completely healed, that it would still take a couple of weeks to do so, but that it would be as good as new when it does. Also, they will give you injections for the pain during the next couple of days, because it will hurt a lot.'

'I had no idea they could do this kind of thing. I wonder if Whitehall knows.' He looked at his arm, turning it back and forth, but then remembered the woman had been hurt as well and blushed. 'I'm sorry, how about you? Did they take care of you too?'

'They put some cream on my face and I feel almost as good as new.' She turned her head to show him that the bruise on her cheek had faded to a dull yellow and was barely visible in the early morning light.

'What about your teeth?'

Tanya grinned, showing him the gap. 'They have good medicines, but apparently they're not very good dentists.' She chuckled. 'Actually, they are, but I do not warrant such special care as you.'

'I'm sorry.'

'Don't worry, I will get some new ones when I get back to Moscow.'

'You're from Moscow? I thought you said Nobo something?'

She shook her head. 'Novosibirsk, it's in Siberia and that's just where my family has a hunting lodge. And you? Are you from London?'

'No, my family's estate is near Oxford.'

'Estate?' Tanya frowned. 'Does that mean you are rich?'

Drake nodded solemnly. 'Very.'

Tanya smiled in satisfaction. 'Then you can pay for some lovely gold teeth for me.'

'On top of the reward from my parents?'

'Of course! Deal?'

She stuck her hand out and Drake laughed as he shook it. 'Deal!'

'Good! Now, I need to pee, so you need to look the other way.' She gave his hand a hard squeeze, then let it go and got to her feet, but her legs gave out and she stumbled and fell onto him.

They froze, staring into each other's eyes, but then, as if realising exactly what position she was in, she blushed and pushed herself off him. She flopped back down on her bed and yawned, rubbing her face, acting as if nothing had happened. 'On second thoughts, I think I'll just stay here a while.'

'Did you get much sleep?'

She shook her head. 'The doctors were working on you for a long time. They brought you here only a couple of hours ago.'

Drake smiled. 'You could have left me and come to bed.'

'If you keep telling me to leave you, one of these days I will!' She laughed, then waved away the suggestion with a sneer. 'They may be good doctors, but they're still Prussians and I don't trust them - I was *not* going to leave you alone with them.

'Thank you.'

'Don't thank me, just buy me something expensive to thank me when we get home.'

Drake laughed incredulously. 'Something else? You've only just asked me to pay for gold teeth! Is this the only reason you're taking care of me?'

'Why else?' She grinned at him. 'It's not as if you're much of a pilot or very pretty, after all, you only shot down one Baron and Gruber is much better looking than you.'

Drake winced. 'Ow. That hurt more than my arm.'

She laughed, but then suddenly turned serious. She slid across the small gap between the beds to sit next to him and looked into his eyes earnestly. 'Did you see the photographs in Gruber's office? On the wall, next to his desk.'

'The ones of aircraft? I didn't get a good look at them, no.'

'They were bad quality and it was hard to make them out, but they were of the Misfit aircraft in the hangars at Vaenga.'

'Are you sure? I mean, you arrived the night before we were shot down, right? You can't have seen them well enough...'

Tanya shook her head, cutting him off. 'There have been drawings of those aircraft in the newspapers every so often for the six months, with all the news of the battle you fought over Britain. And ever since you came here there have been daily articles of the fighting on this front, with representations by our best artists of the kills the Misfits and the Wolfpack have made together. I can assure you, every Muscovite knows exactly what they look like.'

Drake found himself quite glad that he wasn't a Misfit; he wouldn't like to have his every move scrutinised like it had been by the British over the summer and now apparently by the Muscovite public as well. However, at the same time a lump rose in his throat. 'So there's a spy at Vaenga and Gruber knows where the Misfits are based.'

Tanya nodded vigorously. 'Exactly! He could attack them at any time!'

Drake stared at the floor, deeply disturbed.

Vaenga was deep into Muscovite territory and defended by dozens of anti-aircraft batteries in the surrounding woods, but that was no defence against the waves of bombers the Prussians could send. Britain was proof of that; it had taken the entirety of the RAC to stop London from being devastated and here it was only the Misfits and a few ragtag Muscovite squadrons standing in their way.

Would that be a tactic Gruber would use, though? Would he prefer to beat the Misfits in the sky, or would he take any victory that he could get?

Drake hoped that the man would be arrogant enough to want to fight the Misfits himself, but who knew what he would decide to do if the battle starting going against him as it had over the summer.

If only there were some way to get a message out.

CHAPTER 8

There wasn't much more to be said, so Tanya staggered back to her bed. She was snoring as soon as her head hit the hard, bare mattress, but Drake couldn't sleep; his already feverish mind was going round and round in circles, trying to work out what he could possibly do to warn the Misfits. To warn Gwen. He ran through each and every scenario he could think of, but discarded them all as impossible or downright absurd and just ended up making himself feel more frustrated and trapped.

He must have dozed off at some point because the next he knew a guard was standing over him, shouting at him in German to get out of bed.

He jerked awake and rolled onto his feet, blinking away his sleepiness and trying to get his bearings, then gazed around.

Tanya was already being frogmarched out of the room and he made to follow her, but the guard stopped him with a hand to the chest. Another guard stepped forward and threw something on the bed, then pointed at it and said "clothes" in heavily accented English.

Drake eyed the pile of blue cloth - it looked like an RAC officer's day uniform. He nodded at the guard and smiled. 'They are indeed. Well done.'

The guard snarled and stepped forward, raising his hand, but the other spoke before he could strike. 'Don't. Gruber wants him in one piece.'

The guard hesitated at the words, but Drake flinched back from him and held up his hands protectively anyway, pretending not to have understood. 'Alright, alright! I'll put them on!'

He turned away from them in order to hide his smile, filing away the information about Gruber for later, and began undoing his red jumpsuit.

He could tell the uniform was just a copy by the feel of the material and the fact that the rank stripes were not quite in the right place, but it was good to be back in a proper uniform. It felt like he'd regained a measure of his dignity, after the ignominy of capture and imprisonment, and he held his head up just a little bit higher as he was escorted out.

The cell turned out to be the last of a dozen or more, on either side of a long corridor in a low building, one of the new military ones. He couldn't detect any signs of life in any of the others as he passed, though, and he wondered if he and Tanya were the only prisoners. Through a door at the end of the corridor was a small guard room with a desk. Another soldier was there and he exchanged a few words with Drake's guards, making a note on a clipboard, before unlocking the outer door for them.

Drake pulled his greatcoat tightly around him as the guards marched him down the concrete path between the cell block and the neighbouring building and out onto the perimeter track, not for the first time wishing that he had been able to enjoy the Muscovite parka for just a bit longer.

In the light of day it was immediately apparent that the Prussians had taken over and expanded some kind of private air club for their aerodrome, much like what the Misfits had done with a holiday camp in Kent for their base. The brick buildings were what remained of that, but there were also a couple of beautiful, ornately decorated, wrought iron hangars on the other side of the field. They were dwarfed by the recent Prussian constructions and were now sitting abandoned and rusting, slowly losing their splendour, but they were a clear indication of how exclusive the club must have been.

There were signs of recent damage everywhere - unpainted silver patches among the green camouflage of the military buildings, of which the cell block was one, and multiple pockmarks and broken windows on the brick buildings, one of which was completely burnt out - and Drake realised that the air base was the one that the Misfits and Wolfpack had mounted a joint raid on.

By all reports the base had been left in a shambles, with every single fighter a wreck, the buildings damaged, and the field pitted and holed, but the Prussians had shown their usual efficiency and rebuilt, replacing all of the aircraft and patching up the buildings and air field. In double-quick time the aerodrome was operating at peak efficiency once more and, as the guard ushered Drake along, a flight of MU9's began taxiing in an orderly fashion out of the leftmost hangar and lined up for the morning's mission. They were followed closely by MU10's from two other hangars. There was no sign of the Barons, though - the fourth hangar was closed, with no movement evident - and he wondered whether they had gone up already or if Gruber liked to have a bit of a lie in.

He would have liked to watch the Prussians take off, wondering how their drill differed from the British, but he was starting to feel the cold - it wasn't just that his greatcoat was inadequate, but his thermal underwear had been taken away when they'd arrived - so he was glad when they turned off the path and climbed the steps up to the door of one of the smaller brick buildings. The sign on the wall by the door announced it as the pilot's mess, so he wasn't surprised to see Gruber within. The Prussian was reading a newspaper in an armchair in front of a roaring fire, midway down the room, and he looked up when Drake come in and waved with a smile, then motioned towards a table near him.

As he made his way across the room, Drake glanced around curiously. It was about ten yards wide by twenty deep and luxuriously appointed, as if it were a country lodge. There was a bar at the far end with two large tables in front of it, which were occupied by half a dozen pilots in grey Fliegertruppe uniforms, who were eating while trying not to look like they were watching him. The rest of the space was taken up by a dozen armchairs, loosely grouped around the fire, and half a dozen small round tables, like the one that Gruber had pointed to, each seating two to four people.

There was an air of impermanence about the mess, quite unlike any other he'd seen. The only decorations in evidence were paintings of Finnish landscapes and old photographs of smiling people in front of antiquated aircraft, inherited no doubt from the previous occupants. There were no trophies, no portraits of lost pilots, no awards. The squadron colours weren't even on display, something which would be unthinkable in a British squadron.

He idly wondered where the Crimson Barons, part of an invading force, would keep its trophies if they didn't carry them with them. Did they have a home base in Prussia where they sent them for safe keeping?

Gruber met Drake at the table and held his hand out, completely ignoring the guards, who saluted then backed away. 'Thank you for joining me. I apologise for the early hour, but I have a sortie in an hour and I prefer not to fly on an empty stomach.'

The Prussian's black day uniform was severe and functional, the trousers sharply-pressed and the tunic plain, aside from the silver wings on his chest, the epaulettes with gold braid surrounding a single brass star denoting his rank of Generalleutnant (a pay grade higher than Dorothy Campbell) and a black cross hanging from a red ribbon around his throat.

Drake flashed him his best lopsided grin, the one that he knew infuriated self-important people. 'No need to apologise; the sun has been up for at least half an hour. This isn't at all early for a pilot in this war.'

Gruber blinked, momentarily lost for words as he tried to work out whether he was being insulted or not, but his smile didn't falter as he released Drake's hand and went to his seat.

A steward in a white uniform took Drake's greatcoat, then held his chair for him. Only when he was settled did another approach with a large silver tray balanced on his hand and begin to lay food and drink on the table.

'I hope you don't mind, but I took the liberty of instructing the chef to prepare you an English breakfast. If you would prefer something else then just ask. Myself, I'm used to a very American diet.'

While Gruber's plate was filled with things that looked very sweet and not particularly nutritional, including a stack of pancakes, inches tall and dripping in syrup, Drake's was piled with enough bacon, eggs, sausages and toast for several people. He also had a large pot of tea to himself, while Gruber had coffee.

'This is fine, thank you.' Drake nodded gratefully at the steward, who gave him a slight bow in return before retiring. 'Is Praporshik Guseva not joining us?'

Gruber paused with an immense forkful of pancakes half-way to his mouth and stared at him, almost in disbelief. 'Of course not! I want to enjoy a civilised breakfast with you, like two gentlemen, without the inane warbling of a woman to distract from our conversation. Anyway, she is better off eating with her own kind.'

Drake would have liked to protest, but Gruber evidently thought there was nothing more to be said on the subject and started shovelling his food into his mouth as if he were a starving man, barely taking the time to chew before swallowing. He smiled widely between mouthfuls, like a child, not bothering to wipe the syrup from his chin.

Drake hurriedly looked away from the revolting sight and began eating in a far more dignified fashion, extremely relieved that he had the use of both arms, saving him the indignity of having someone cut his food up for him, or, horror of horrors, forgo manners and use the fork in his right hand. Like Gruber was. He cut a half-inch slice from one of the thin Prussian sausages and chewed fastidiously; just because he was among barbarians didn't mean he couldn't still be civilised.

'So, how shall we address each other? Will you insist on your title?'

Gruber spoke around a mouthful and once more Drake had to fight to contain his disgust at the man's poor table manners.

'Of course not; that was just for your underling. However, I don't think we're quite on a first name basis, especially given the circumstances. Perhaps, despite the advantage you have over me,' Drake nodded at the gold on the man's shoulder boards, 'we should stick with ranks.'

Gruber nodded reluctantly. 'Very well, that is acceptable for now, although I hope you and I can become friends at some point.'

Drake shrugged. 'After Britain has won the war and things go back to how they should be, that might be possible, I suppose.'

A brief flash of anger darkened Gruber's face, but it was gone in an instant.

Drake pretended not to see it while he concentrated on his food, but he stored the man's short temper away with the other information he'd gleaned, like the fact that Gruber seemed to be keeping himself isolated from his pilots and, by the looks they were shooting his way, they didn't particularly like him.

Gruber showed his training as an actor by continuing on as if Drake hadn't said something that had disagreed with him. 'I assume you are in Russia to train pilots to fly your Harridans.'

Drake considered what to do. Under the terms of war he was under no obligation to tell Gruber anything and if he did he could get in serious trouble from his own government, but, considering the man had a spy in Vaenga, he probably wasn't asking anything that he didn't already know. And besides, by talking to the man he might be able to worm his way into his confidence, which might come in handy at a later date.

He nodded. 'I was brought over to give the Muscovites a bit of a hand, yes.'

'Muscovites.' Gruber chuckled, spraying flecks of food on the table, and shook his head. 'As if a change of name will make a difference to who they really are - Imperialists with a thirst for territory. It's merely a political stunt to curry favour with you British. Once they no longer need you, or if they make other... *arrangements*, the name will revert and so will they.' He gave Drake a sly grin.

Drake raised an eyebrow. 'I think you will be surprised at how determined they are *not* to make any arrangements with you. If you've read any history books, you'll know they don't take very kindly to invaders and they don't bow to them, no matter how much it costs.'

'We shall see, but anyway, we were talking about you before we got sidetracked.' With a squeal of his fork, Gruber scraped his plate clean of the last traces of pancake, then stuck them in his mouth. To Drake's relief, he swallowed before speaking again, though. 'So, tell me, who did you annoy to get sent to this godforsaken place?'

'Nobody, I volunteered. I was starting to get a bit bored, just twiddling my thumbs in England after we beat you, and was looking for something to do.'

'Well, I'm afraid you got a little bit more excitement than you bargained for!'

The Prussian chuckled as he began tucking into a pastry and Drake took the opportunity to eat more himself. He was extremely hungry, not having eaten anything since before being lured into the Muscovite bunker, and it was all he could do to restrain himself from joining Gruber in wolfing down the food.

'Tell me about Gwen Stone.'

Gruber's voice was low and casual, his face innocent, and he kept his eyes on his food as if the question were of no importance to him, but Drake could still tell this was where Gruber had wanted to take the conversation all along. He chewed carefully, using it as an excuse for not speaking straight away, giving himself time to wonder why the man would ask such a thing. Had his spy seen him with Gwen? Did he know about their past?

He swallowed, then very deliberately wiped his mouth clean with his napkin before answering. 'She's one of the Misfit pilots.'

'Any fool who has read an English newspaper knows that.' Gruber scoffed and waved at a rack of newspapers at the side of the room next to the entrance. From where Drake was sitting he could see there were a few British newspapers among the Prussian ones. 'I even received a letter from her personally.' Gruber smirked when Drake's eyes widened in surprise. 'You did not know? I thought your *childhood friend* would tell you something like that. Or have the two of you drifted apart? Mr F Featherstonehaugh's articles make no mention of that, in fact he said that you two were very close, especially on board the *Arturo*.'

Drake couldn't help but grit his teeth, showing his frustration; the insistence of the British press on reporting things that should remain hushed up, at least until they bloody well didn't matter, could very well have dumped him in hot water.

A look of satisfaction at Drake's reaction briefly passed across Gruber's face, but again it disappeared quickly and returned to his amiable mask.

While Drake was annoyed, he couldn't help but be puzzled as well; he had no idea how his relationship with Gwen could possibly be of any interest to Gruber. He nodded reluctantly. 'You're right, Gwen and I were friends a long time ago, but we lost contact with each other. Before the Arturo we hadn't seen each other for more than a decade.'

'Then you must have had a lot to catch up on.'

'Yes. We did.' Drake nodded, then looked back down at his plate. He delicately placed some of his remaining fried egg onto a piece of toast, then cut a small mouthful of it, before spearing it and delivering it to his mouth without displacing a crumb. His mother would have been proud, but, at that moment, manners weren't what were important to him - it was the time he was taking over them which was giving him a chance for his racing mind to frantically run through everything he knew about Gwen, to see if there was anything he shouldn't reveal. For the life of him he couldn't find anything.

With the food still in his mouth, he looked up at Gruber again and found the man leaning back in his chair, watching him, his hand wrapped around a large cup of black coffee. There was a confident smile on the man's face, as if he knew something that Drake didn't, and he tried to keep his chewing regular, even as his heart skipped a beat.

Unable to delay any more, he finally swallowed. 'Why are you so interested in Gwen? I would have thought you'd want to know more about Abby, or Owen, or even Scarlet.'

'You're right, of course; as a pilot she isn't up to much...'

'She beat you.' Drake couldn't help throwing the comment out, then kicked himself; the last thing he should be doing was provoking Gruber, but he found he couldn't just sit by and let the man disparage his friend.

Surprisingly, Gruber didn't take offence, but nodded in acknowledgement. 'That is perfectly true, *but*,' he held up a finger to punctuate the word, 'that was because of her aircraft, not because of any superior skill on her part. I assure you that it was an anomaly and it won't happen again; *I* now have the superior machine. You have seen Hölle in action - even you must admit that it is far superior to Flamme, better even than Wasp or Dragonfly.'

'Perhaps, but I still think you are underestimating Gwen's talents as a pilot.'

'Perhaps.' Gruber threw the word back at him. 'However, today we begin our assault on Murmansk itself. I have no doubt the Misfits will be there and we shall have ample opportunity to find out.' He tipped his head back, draining the dregs of his coffee, then wiped his mouth with his napkin and tossed it on the table. 'Well, this has been pleasant, but I'm afraid I have to go. We will speak again, perhaps over dinner tonight? I'm sure there will be plenty to celebrate.'

Gruber stood and gave Drake a smile. 'Until later, then.'

He walked out without a backwards glance and Drake wasn't surprised when two heavy hands descended on his shoulders.

He smiled up into the faces of the two scowling guards and waved a hand at his plate. 'Would you mind awfully waiting while I finish?'

CHAPTER 9

With Gruber gone, Drake's status had evidently reverted back from guest to prisoner and the guards hadn't felt like standing around while Drake enjoyed the rest of his meal. They all but pulled him out of his seat and began shoving him towards the door, but the disdainful sniff of the steward, who had served the two pilots, held them at bay long enough for him to help Drake into his coat. He barely had time to give the man a grateful nod, before he was propelled to the door and out into the cold.

The MU9's and 10's were long gone, but the doors of the fourth hangar were open and Drake caught sight of men working within on the red aircraft of the Barons, preparing them for the morning's sortie. He tried to linger to get a better look, but the guards were having none of it and hurried him back to his cell with only a quick detour to the medical centre for an injection.

Tanya was already there and, by the way she was sitting on the edge of her bed, biting her lip, Drake could tell she had something to tell him and it was most likely not good. Her news had to wait, though, because the guards made Drake change out of the ersatz RAC uniform and back into the red jumpsuit first.

When the Prussians finally left the room, Drake sat on his bed and looked at her inquisitively, but she motioned for him to wait and tilted her head, listening. It was only when the footsteps of the guards had completely faded away and the door at the end of the corridor had slammed shut, that she smiled at him. 'Sorry, I didn't want an audience.'

'Why? What's wrong? I assume from what Gruber told me you were having breakfast with fellow Muscovites, right?'

'I was, yes. Although, cabbage stew isn't exactly my idea of breakfast.'

'I'm sorry.'

She waved away his apology. 'It doesn't matter. While the food was disgusting, it did mean that I could catch up with what's been happening while we've been wandering around in the forest.'

'Hang on. Before you start...' When he'd put his coat back on after getting changed he thought he'd felt something and he put his hands in his pockets and found several objects. From his right he pulled out several chocolate bars, Belgian, thankfully, and not the awful Prussian stuff, which he threw on the bed, but in the left he found a napkin knotted around three jam-filled Danish pastries.

Tanya squealed and leapt from the bed. She snatched one of the pastries and immediately bit into it, groaning in ecstasy. Too late she realised what she'd done and looked at him. 'You don't mind, do you?'

For some reason it was far more endearing when Tanya spoke around a mouthful of food than when Gruber had done so.

'Not at all.' Drake shook his head and held out the rest of the pastries with a grin.

'Thank you!' She smiled happily as she snatched them and took them to her bed.

After his huge breakfast, Drake wasn't hungry, so he contented himself with watching her, silently thanking the steward for his kindness, and only spoke when she started work on the last one. 'So, what was the news? Let me guess. The Prussians have overrun the border and are pushing on Murmansk.'

Tanya glared at him, pouting in mock irritation as she swallowed a last morsel. 'If you know everything already I'm just going to catch up on the sleep I missed taking care of you.'

Drake chuckled. 'I'm sorry. *Please*. Tell me what you found out.'

Tanya grunted, tossing her head exaggeratedly and turning away from him. 'I'm not sure I want to.'

'Please? I'll buy you something even nicer when we get to England?'

She turned back and grinned at him. 'Alright!'

Drake laughed as she leapt off her bed again and flopped down next to him.

Her happiness at the prospect of more expensive gifts from an English Lord vanished, though, when she began her report. 'A couple of days after we were shot down, the Prussians crossed the border.

They blasted straight through our lines as if they weren't there and drove deep into Muscovy. Almost half the Muscovite troops were killed or captured in the initial push and the rest were forced to retreat in disarray. So many of my countrymen have been captured in fact that they don't have anywhere to put them. The ones on this base are overflow from Prussian army camps, waiting for transport to more permanent facilities in places like Finland and Poland.'

'That's not good.'

Tanya raised an eyebrow at his very British understatement. 'No, it isn't, but that's not the end of the story. Most of the soldiers here were captured during that initial attack, but there are a few that were brought in later and they have a very different story to tell.' She grinned. 'Apparently, the Prussians had no idea how to deal with the cold and got bogged down after only a day or two. Some of the soldiers I spoke to had stones and canteens thrown at them because the enemy's rifles wouldn't work and there are also reports of entire patrols being found frozen to death in the snow.'

Drake smiled at her glee, understanding it completely; the Prussians were getting what they deserved: the same treatment every other invader of Russia had received over the centuries - the vengeance of the land itself.

'Unfortunately it didn't last very long. The Prussians learnt fairly quickly and they were supported by Finns coming up from the south - the ones we found in the bunker were probably left behind to secure their rear. The Muscovites were forced to retreat again, but this time it was far more organised. A few of the men and women I spoke to were part of the rearguard and they said that the majority of the remaining forces had made it across the river and were going to concentrate their forces at Murmansk. They're fairly optimistic that they'll be able to hold out because they have the Misfits to support them until the weather closes in, which is supposed to happen sometime in the next few days.'

Drake nodded. 'Let's hope they're right, otherwise the Prussians will have their hands on the northern passage and all this effort will have been in vain.'

'Yes.' Tanya nodded sincerely. 'Oh, one last thing - all the Muscovite prisoners are dressed in blue jumpsuits, we're the only ones in red.'

'And they're all soldiers? No pilots among them?'

'No. None whatsoever.'

'Well, it no longer looks like we're going to be summarily executed just for being pilots, but now we have the mystery of why we're being segregated from the other prisoners and why we're the only ones in red.'

'I guess we'll find out sometime.' Tanya shrugged, not seeming too concerned. 'So, how was your breakfast? Did you find out anything else apart from that they're attacking Murmansk today?'

'My breakfast was much tastier than yours by the sound of things, but I must say that the company left much to be desired.'

'I can imagine.' She nodded, sincerely. 'I've never liked Gruber, even in the films where he was supposed to be playing the good guy; he's too smarmy, too sure of himself. I prefer British films, where the star is shy and doesn't know he's a hero, even when he wins.' She winked. 'A bit like you, really.'

Drake shook his head. 'I'm no hero.'

'See?'

Drake stared at her, searching for traces of sarcasm and was quite shocked when he didn't find any. He didn't consider himself a hero, but he knew that many people back home saw fighter pilots as such, especially since the events of the battle in the skies over Britain, when the newspapers had made it sound like the only thing keeping the Kaiser and his hordes at bay were a few men and women in small, fragile fighter aircraft.

He had no idea what to say in reply, but he was saved from the necessity when the whir of airscrews cutting through the air came from outside.

As one, they leapt up onto Drake's bed to peer through the high-level window.

By squashing their cheeks against the window and craning their heads they could make out a small slice of the airfield beyond the neighbouring brick building and they were just in time to see flashes of red as the Barons took off.

The sound of the airscrews faded quickly and Drake stepped off the bed, but Tanya stayed in place just long enough to spit a few words in Russian. He raised an eyebrow at her when she sat back down and she shrugged. 'I wished them well in their mission.'

The laughter Tanya's comment provoked didn't last long and the conversation petered out not long after as exhaustion made its presence felt. The Muscovite woman soon went back to her own bed and the two of them wrapped themselves in their coats and fell asleep.

Drake woke some time later to the noise of first the MU9's and MU10's coming back, then to the return of the Barons. He wasn't positive, but each time it seemed that each time there were far fewer aircraft returning than had taken off and the thought gave him some small comfort.

At midday, two metal plates were shoved under the door. This time they both had the same food - bread, water, sausage and, to Tanya's disgust, more cabbage. Drake didn't mind the cabbage too much, though; it reminded him of school dinners. They supplemented the meal with the last of Drake's rations from the survival kit, leaving it completely empty apart from a few scraps of bandages, empty flasks and the penknife, and shared one of the Belgian chocolate bars as dessert.

With nothing better to do, they slept the whole afternoon into the early evening and were only vaguely aware when the fighters went up again.

A few hours of fitful sleep weren't nearly enough to make up for almost a week of walking the nights away and shivering through days, though, and Drake wasn't feeling particularly rested when the lights flared on, the cell door banged against the wall and guards burst in.

Tanya was pulled out of bed and shoved against the wall out of the way by one of the Prussians, while another held out a pile of clothes to Drake and told him to get changed. This time it was a dress uniform they had brought him, which went a long way to explain the care with which the guards gave it to him and their unusual patience while they waited for Drake to put it on. Once more, the uniform wasn't quite right: the material was slightly rougher than the official one he'd gotten from his tailor on Savile Row; the RAC insignia on the breast of the long, form-fitting tunic was a cheap, brassy copy and not the gold-plaited one he'd paid extra for, as were the buttons; the purple band on the top hat wasn't *quite* the right shade; the shiny black riding boots were about a half-size too big; and of course he was without the medals he'd won in France and Britain. It did fit him almost as well as his own did, though, thankfully, and he shuddered to think what he would have looked like if the, already tight, riding breeches hadn't been exactly the right size.

There was no mirror handy for him to check his appearance, but Tanya's admiring look was all the confirmation he needed that he made a dashing picture and he gave her one of his most charming smiles as he was grabbed, surprisingly lightly, and rushed from the cell.

Drake was met at the door of the pilot's mess by the steward from breakfast, who welcomed him with a short bow and helped him out of his coat. He thanked the man, holding his eye a fraction more than was necessary to make sure he knew it wasn't just the current service he was grateful for. The steward gave him a corresponding fraction of a nod in return, before disappearing with the coat into an adjoining cloakroom. When he returned a few seconds later he dismissed the guards with a cool nod then preceded Drake into the room.

Gruber was in his armchair by the fire, perusing a newspaper, but as soon as he caught sight of Drake, he tossed the paper to one side and came towards him.

The Prussian was likewise wearing dress uniform for the evening and it was as impressive as it was imposing. His tunic was black and form-fitting, giving him wide shoulders and a slim waist, and had silver buttons in a single line down the front, each embossed with death's heads. A crimson lanyard went over his right shoulder under the stiff, gold braid-covered rank board and the same iron cross on red ribbon was around his neck and in addition there were more than a dozen medals, of various sizes and shapes, pinned to his breast, which made Drake feel the lack of his own ones even more acutely. Finishing off the ensemble were pressed black trousers, which were much tighter than they should be, tucked into highly-polished black calf-length boots that reflected the candlelight in the room like mirrors.

'Welcome! Thank you for joining us tonight, on this most auspicious of occasions.' Gruber smiled widely and grabbed Drake's hand, shaking it heartily.

Drake extracted his hand from the man's clammy grasp as soon as he could and raised an eyebrow. 'Auspicious? What are we celebrating? Some Prussian festival that I've never heard of? As far as I know it's not October...'

'Ha ha! Such wonderful British humour!'

Drake was amazed when the man actually seemed to genuinely laugh at his feeble joke; either he had already started on the schnapps or something had happened to make the man overlook any digs that Drake might make at him.

'No, no, I will not spoil the surprise. First we will eat and drink, then all will be revealed later. Come!'

Gruber put his arm companionably around Drake's shoulder and pulled him further into the room.

The mess had been transformed since breakfast. Gone were the small tables and chairs and in their place were the two long ones, pushed together to make a single dining table. They were covered with a white lace cloth and laid with expensive-looking china and silverware, including very distinct, very ornate, silver candelabra, which seemed vaguely familiar to Drake.

Gruber saw the direction of his gaze and grinned. 'Ah ha! I *knew* you'd seen my movies! They're the candlesticks from the wedding scene of "The Baron and the Princess", replicas of course, made by a silversmith in Berlin; the ones in the flick were only chicken wire and tin foil. Don't worry, I won't be whipping out my sword and cutting the candles in half tonight, but only because decent candles are far too hard to come across out here in the wilds!'

He laughed heartily and Drake smiled politely, all the time wondering if he should tell the man that he'd never seen any of his pictures and that the only reason he'd recognised the candlesticks was that they'd featured quite prominently on the poster that had been plastered all over every cinema in England during the run of the flyvie. He decided it was better not to say anything, at least not before dinner, and instead looked around at the other men that would be joining them for the meal. They were all pilots, but dressed in the more usual storm cloud grey dress uniforms of Die Fliegertruppe. Drake was interested to note that only six of them had a red lanyard like Gruber's, evidently marking them as Crimson Barons - it seemed that they had been whittled down a bit since he'd faced them, probably by the Misfits.

'Ah, yes, let me introduce you.' Gruber led Drake to the head of the table and placed him at his right hand, in the spot of the guest of honour. 'This is Oberst Schwarz, he commands the MU9 and MU10 squadrons.' He indicated the man standing behind the chair immediately to his left, who clicked his heels together smartly and gave a short sharp bow.

'Pleasure to meet you, Lord Drake.'

Schwarz was in his early thirties, young for his rank and responsibility, with jet black hair, slicked severely back. Unlike Gruber, he wasn't smiling, instead there was a weariness and sorrow in his eyes that betrayed the fact that he was of the opinion that there was nothing to be celebrating. Looking around the table, Drake could easily see why; with the MU9's, 10's and Barons there were at least three squadrons on the base, if not more, but there were only twenty three pilots standing stiffly around the table, waiting for Gruber to take his seat - not enough to fill even two squadrons. They wouldn't have come with anything less than a full complement of pilots so they must have lost a fair number in the fighting in the north.

Drake couldn't bring himself to feel sorry for the man, or his pilots, though; they were his enemy and the fewer there were of them the better.

'The honour is all mine, Oberst Schwarz.' Drake gave him a respectful nod in return; Gruber was a decent pilot, but he was essentially nothing more than a figurehead. He hadn't done anything to actually *earn* his rank or position, beyond be famous enough to make good propaganda and his success was mostly due to the full resources of the Prussian Empire being handed to him on a plate. Schwarz, on the other hand, would have had to prove his worth and would have done so with only the tools that the rest of the Prussian pilots had - a mass-produced aircraft and skill.

After Drake had greeted the man, Gruber waved vaguely at the rest of the pilots gathered around the table. 'There's no need for me to introduce anyone else, so let's just eat; I'm starving!' He sat and immediately waved for a wine waiter.

Drake raised an eyebrow at the abysmal manners, but caught the Oberst looking at him and quickly made his expression neutral. The man was obviously in agreement with Drake's assessment, though, because he gave him the minutest of shrugs in return, before taking his seat.

The food was wonderful, but the meal was almost as intolerable as Drake had feared it would be and, if it hadn't been for the refined and dignified presence of Schwarz to counter Gruber's crudeness, which only became more so as the night went on and the actor consumed more and more wine, Drake would most likely have punched the man and hang the consequences. Gruber truly was a bore in every sense of the word: he was self-aggrandising and exceedingly tiresome, needing to be the centre of attention at all times, cutting off everyone who tried to get a word in edgewise and insulting anyone who dared to have a differing opinion to him. It was patently obvious why his pilots kept themselves at a distance from him in the mess and Drake had the horrible feeling that his callousness and disregard for them might continue when it came time to fight.

However, during the whole interminable ordeal, nothing was said about the reason for the celebration and it wasn't until after desert had been consumed and Gruber was lounging back in his chair with a cigar in one hand and a vodka martini in the other that the subject was broached.

'Well, we had quite an interesting day, didn't we boys?' Gruber grinned and looked around the table. The lower-ranked Prussians all dutifully laughed, agreeing with him, but Drake noted that none of them was particularly enthusiastic or sincere about it. Gruber carried on regardless, though, and Drake wondered if he didn't notice or just didn't care.

'We flew a good few sorties today, in support of the forces at Murmansk and, while the Muscovites did manage to repel the attacks, they have expended all their limited resources in doing so and I'm certain that tomorrow we will take the city.' Gruber took a drag on his cigar while he paused to let the information sink in, all the while watching for Drake's reaction.

Drake didn't give him the satisfaction and just raised an eyebrow. 'Oh? Well, I think your celebration might be a little bit premature, old boy, they may yet pull something out of the hat and surprise you.'

'I think not,' Gruber waved away the notion with a derogatory smirk, 'but anyway, that isn't what we're here for.' He signalled to a waiter, who came forwards with something flat and heavy, covered by a white cloth, which he placed in front of Gruber.

The leader of the Barons didn't touch it, though, he just set his hands on the table either side of it and smiled at Drake. 'This morning we had a run-in with the Misfits.'

Drake nodded. 'That's not exactly surprising.' He smiled apologetically at Schwarz and the rest of the pilots around the table. 'Your reduced numbers told me as much.'

'That is of no consequence; there are plenty more pilots to be had.' Again Gruber waved away Drake's comment. 'What's important is this.'

He whipped back the white cloth dramatically to reveal a piece of scratched and charred metal.

Drake stared at it in horror. 'No...'

The word was scarcely more than a whisper, but Gruber heard and his smile widened in glee.

In itself, the piece of Duralumin could have come from just about any aircraft, but the traces of paint left on it, in an unmistakable shade of pink, declared its origin without a doubt.

Drake still couldn't believe it, though, and shook his head in denial. 'It can't be true.'

Gruber grinned. 'I'm afraid so.' He picked up the piece of metal and turned it over in his hands careful not to cut himself on the jagged and twisted edges. 'I shot down Wasp during this morning's sortie. This is the only part we could find, the rest is at the bottom of the river near Murmansk.'

'And...' Drake's voice hitched and he gulped down some water before continuing. 'And Gwen? Did she get out?'

Gruber shrugged, as if he didn't care either way. 'She did, but she was very low. I thought she was too low to survive, but I'm informed that she did, although she was hurt quite badly.'

Drake looked from Gruber to the chunk of Duralumin and finally to Schwarz. 'Please tell me this is just some sort of game and he's lying.'

Schwarz shook his head solemnly. 'He's not. I'm sorry.'

Drake glared at Gruber. He found he was angry suddenly and all the good manners in the world weren't going to stop him showing it. 'Is this why you invited me to dinner? To taunt me with this?'

Gruber took a deep drag on his cigar, then stubbed the rest out before answering. 'Of course not. Why on earth would I want to do that? I merely thought that you were bound to find out about this sooner or later and would want to know that your friend survived the ordeal, that is all.' He downed the rest of his martini, then stood. 'Now, if you will excuse me, I have things to do before bed and a sortie to fly in the morning.'

The steward from earlier helped Gruber on with his overcoat, which matched his uniform for colour, then, without even a glance at his men, Gruber picked up the piece of metal and left.

With Gruber gone, the other pilots seemed almost to melt in their seats and normal conversation started up.

Drake was in no mood to join in with it, even if they had tried to include him, and it was almost a relief when two guards approached the table, their attention firmly fixed on him.

He shoved his chair back, more than ready to go with them, but Oberst Schwarz stood and waved them away. 'Would you allow me the honour of escorting you back to your quarters, Lord Drake?'

Drake was taken by surprise by the man's offer, coming as it was after a night in which he had dined well but been treated poorly. His first instinct was to refuse point blank and turn his back on the whole damn lot of them, but he managed to stop himself before he said something irrevocable and reconsidered.

On the surface it seemed to be just a courteous gesture, one a gentleman might well make to a guest, but then he remembered how there had been something in the Oberst's eyes that told Drake that he hadn't been getting the whole story about how Gwen had been shot down and he realised that the man might well want to get him alone to tell him.

He nodded and smiled genuinely for the first time since the meal had begun. 'I would be delighted, thank you.'

A steward helped Drake into his shabby greatcoat and the two men stepped out into the night with the guards followed at a discreet distance.

At first they just walked in silence along the perimeter track, taking the long way back to the cells, enjoying the clear night even though it was desperately cold. However, after a couple of minutes the man gave the guards a covert glance, as if to make sure that they were out of earshot and, without any preamble, began to talk.

'One of Generalleutnant Gruber's Karmesinroten Barone came to see me after this morning's flight, wanting to file a report against his commander.'

Drake stared at the man. He'd thought he'd get a comment on Gruber's atrocious behaviour over dinner, or perhaps an apology, but not this.

Schwarz didn't even glance at him, he just remained staring straight ahead as he continued speaking, as if he felt that by doing so he was just talking to the night and not really telling secrets to an enemy.

'The pilot is nominally Gruber's second in command, although whether that actually counts for anything is debatable, and he felt that it was his duty to draw to my attention what actually happened during the sortie.'

Schwarz stopped talking just long enough to return the salute of a group of mechanics as they passed by and Drake noted the respect for the pilot in the men's gestures and body language, something that he hadn't seen demonstrated for Gruber, not even by the stewards in the mess, who were only rigidly polite.

'It didn't particularly surprise me that Herr Gruber didn't tell you the details of how he shot Aerial Officer Stone down because he didn't exactly cover himself in glory. Rather than triumphing in a duel with a worthy opponent, he instead attacked her from the rear as she was firing upon ground forces, taking her by surprise. Now, that in itself is not unusual and I believe you will agree that it is a perfectly understandable tactic of warfare, which I am sure you have used, just as I have.'

Schwarz glanced out of the corner of his eyes at Drake, who merely gave him a confirming nod.

'However, it wasn't so much the manner in which Gruber shot down Wasp that disturbed the man, but rather what happened next which prompted him to come to me.'

Drake went even colder than he already was; there was only one thing Schwarz could possibly be about to say, only one thing that Gruber could possibly have done after destroying Wasp that would have distressed a pilot enough for him to speak out against his commander.

By this time they had arrived at the cell block and Schwartz slowed, then stopped. He turned to Drake for the first time, meeting and holding his gaze with dark eyes. 'Wasp was destroyed at a high enough altitude for Officer Stone to get out without any problem whatsoever, but Gruber made a run at her while she was hanging from her glidewings. She tucked her wings in just as he opened fire and he missed, but she was barely able to redeploy her wings in time and was going very fast when she hit the treetops.'

'Gruber said she was injured badly. Did his spy at Vaenga tell him that?'

Schwarz's eyes widened ever so slightly, the only betrayal of his surprise at Drake's knowledge of the spy's existence and he smiled minutely before nodding. 'Yes. The report came in this evening. Her injuries are consistent with the fall, she was not hit by fire either during Wasp's destruction or after.'

Drake sighed in relief. 'Thank the fates.'

'Indeed.' The man nodded solemnly. 'I have met Officer Stone myself, you know. This was more than ten years ago, at a conference of the *Société Aéronautique* and she was just "Miss Hawking" back then, of course, and accompanied by her parents. She was so very young, but even then one could see her promise. It would be a shame for that promise to go to waste, especially due to the actions of one man who is only thinking of revenge.'

He again glanced at the guards and when he saw that they were at a safe distance his usually impassive face showed a modicum of emotion for the first time. 'Most of us are not the bloodthirsty psychopaths our leaders are, but there are enough men like Gruber to make this war entirely distasteful and far too often they are given the power to do as their dark hearts please.'

'We've got a few of those as well. I think one of them was just made minister for war...'

'I sympathise.' Schwarz's attention was drawn by the guards, who were still keeping their distance, but becoming increasingly nervous, shooting anxious looks their way. 'I'm sorry, my time has run out, but before I leave you I will tell you what I told the pilot - that Gruber's behaviour was reprehensible and against every *unwritten* code, whether

it be between gentlemen or aviators, but there is nothing against it in
the rulebook. So, while I condemn his actions with every fibre of my
being, I am unfortunately not permitted to condemn him through
official channels.'

'That's a shame, but thank you for telling me.'

'No need to thank me; I am only expressing what any man of
conscience would.' He held out his hand and Drake took it, expecting
a simple goodnight, but was shocked when the man sighed and gave
him a look of extreme sorrow. 'I apologise for what will happen to you
after you leave here; nobody deserves that kind of treatment, let alone
a pilot and a gentleman, but it is better than the fate of some and
perhaps you may live through it.'

With that, the man released Drake's hand, nodded to the guards,
then walked back the way they had come.

Gruber left the mess hall and went straight to his office. He lay the
twisted piece of Duralumin reverently in the centre of his desk, then
unpinned several of the photographs from the wall and placed them
next to it. He sat, leaning forwards, propped up on his forearms, and
studied the images for the last time.

He smiled as he took in the smooth, clean lines of Wasp, lines that
had inspired his own beautiful machine and that he had destroyed that
morning.

He allowed himself a couple of minutes to savour the moment, then
he burnt the photographs one by one, crushing their ashes in the metal
waste paper basket under his desk, using the flame from the last to light
his final celebratory cigar of the night.

CHAPTER 10

'What do you think he meant?' Tanya asked when Drake had finished telling her about his conversation with Schwarz.

She hadn't seemed at all surprised by Gruber's attempt to kill Gwen under her glidewings and had even told Drake that she would do the same if it was a Baron in her sights, but his final comment had them both puzzled.

'I don't know. If I get the chance I'll ask him, but I'm afraid we'll find out soon enough.'

'Maybe not.' Tanya grinned. 'I have a cunning plan, my Lord Drake!'

She reached down and pulled a large knife from underneath the mattress of her bed.

'Where on earth did you get that?' He frowned at it. 'That's not one of yours.'

'No, it's not,' she brandished it, making it spin in her hands. 'This is a standard issue Prussian infantry knife.'

'How did you get it?'

'I picked the pocket of a nice Prussian sergeant who likes beating up Muscovite prisoners a little bit too much. Hopefully he'll get in a lot of trouble for losing it.'

'Picked the pocket...? Dare I ask?'

'I was a thief before the war. Didn't you know?' She winked, then slipped the knife back under her mattress. 'Anyway, it's vastly inferior to my blades, but I will make do.'

'Make do for what?'

'Tonight, at about three or four o'clock, when things are nice and quiet, we're going to make a break for it.'

Drake chuckled. 'I don't know if you've noticed, but we're in a cell here.'

'I had noticed that, funnily enough, Rudy.' Tanya rolled her eyes. 'That's why I'm going to use this to pick the lock.' She held up his penknife. 'It's about time it was useful for something after we've carried it so far.'

'Alright...' Drake took a deep breath, preparing to state the obvious once more, but she held up a hand to stop him.

'Yes, I am well aware that we are again behind enemy lines and with the entire Prussian Northern Army between us and Murmansk.'

'Good,' Drake grinned. 'Because I was a tad worried that you'd forgotten.'

'I haven't,' she shook her head earnestly, 'which is why we're going to borrow a couple of their aircraft.'

Drake found himself unable to sleep and he lay staring up at the ceiling, listening to Tanya's regular breathing.

The Muscovite's plan was a bold one, perhaps foolhardy or desperate, but he was fully conscious of the fact that it might well be the last chance they had to escape the Prussians and make it back to Vaenga before the Arturo left. Before Gwen left.

Somehow, though, the prospect of missing the transport back to England was no longer so abhorrent to him, the need to get back to Gwen no longer so urgent, and he glanced across to the woman in the bed next to him, only a few feet away in the cramped room. In the glow from the moonlight coming through the window she almost seemed at peace, although he knew from the few times he had been on watch during the daytime that some part of her was still aware and the slightest activity or thing out of place would bring her instantly awake, knife in hand ready to kill.

As if sensing his gaze, Tanya's eyes opened and her head turned towards him. 'Stop looking at me like that.'

'Like what?'

In reply she just rolled her eyes, then swung out of bed and took the two steps over to him. She lay down in front of him, her back pressed against him. 'Never mind. Just get some sleep.'

She grabbed his arm and pulled it around her.

They had been in close proximity many times since they had first shared warmth, but it had only been for that, for survival. This was different, for comfort, and Drake found his tension washing away and his awareness of the world with it.

'Rudy, come on, time to go.'

Drake opened his eyes to find Tanya's dark shape looming over him, her hand shaking his shoulder gently.

'What...?'

'No questions. Just put your coat on and follow me. Quietly.'

A surge of adrenaline brought Drake instantly awake and he swivelled his legs out of bed. 'What do you need me to do?' he hissed.

'Just what you're told.'

He was about to stand, but stopped when he noticed that the bed was cold where the Muscovite had been next to him and that the cell door was already open. He opened his mouth to ask her about it, but she gave him a look and he closed it again.

She smiled and reached out to pat him on the shoulder. 'Good boy, you're learning at last.'

Drake stifled a laugh, then stood and followed her from the room.

The light from the guardroom at the end of the corridor was warm and inviting, but Drake found his breathing hitching as they neared it, knowing what he would find.

It was worse than he'd imagined.

It didn't matter that he had seen Tanya take apart several men before, seen her stain pure white snow the deepest red, each time was a shock.

Her favoured method for killing Prussians with her knives was from behind, a single cut to the throat severing the arteries while similarly piercing their windpipe and cutting off their ability to cry out, but it seemed that this time she had been unable to take her victim by surprise. Instead of the clinical precision that she had demonstrated previously, there were signs of the Prussian putting up a fight. It had done him no good and only served to prolong the inevitable, but it meant far more wounds than usual and that, combined with the close quarters, meant that almost every surface in the room, the floor, walls, even ceiling, was liberally covered with blood. As was she.

'Come *on*, Rudy!'

Drake started at Tanya's hiss and realised that he had stopped just inside the room to stare at the gory sight. He shook himself out of his stupor and stepped carefully around the pools of blood to join her at the door.

She looked at him inquisitively and he gave her a tense nod in return; this was the most dangerous part of the escape. They had known exactly where the guard was going to be within the cell block, but beyond the door was an unknown - there might be entire patrols walking the paths, drunken soldiers staggering to their barracks, or even dogs.

Tanya opened the door a crack and looked out, blocking as much of the light with her body as possible. She grunted in satisfaction, then slipped through.

Drake followed her and closed the door behind them as softly as he could. He winced as the latch clicked, seeming like a gunshot in the silence of the night, but there was no shout of alarm and he moved to the side of the door, crouching beside it as they had discussed, waiting for her to check the area.

'We're clear.'

Her whisper came from right beside his ear and gave him the shock of his life. He half leapt up, half toppled to the side and tripped over his own feet, ending up sprawled face down on the grass.

He rolled over to find Tanya kneeling beside him, grinning, her teeth white in the faint moonlight.

'Stop messing about, Rudy, and let's go!'

Glad that the darkness hid his blushes, he picked himself up and followed her as she set off at a crouching run between the buildings towards the airfield.

The Prussians had done an extremely good job of clearing the snow from the facility, using the Muscovite prisoners to shovel the places that their machines couldn't reach and the going was far easier than it would have been. It also meant that it would be much harder for them to be seen, their dark figures not standing out against moonlit snow.

They got to the perimeter track and hunkered down to survey the ground at the end of the adjacent building, a barracks by the chorus of snoring coming from within. The direct route to the hangars would take them across the airfield, but that would be suicide; even without snow on the ground, movement in the open would catch the eye of anyone looking even casually in their general direction. The other option was to take the track around the outside of the field. It was a lot further, a mile or more, but once they got past the last of the brick buildings, the trees would hide them much better. As long as they didn't meet any guards coming the other way, of course.

There was nobody around, so Tanya led them at a run along the perimeter track, still hunched over and sticking to the grass alongside the concrete to deaden their footfalls. The buildings they passed were all still, silent and dark, apart for the one on the end, which appeared to be some kind of guard hut or communications shed and from which laughter came every so often.

Tanya grinned at him when they were safely in the clear and they slowed down and began jogging easily. 'I guess we know where the guards are.'

Drake huffed quietly in agreement, but didn't have the breath to answer properly; he was still feeling the effects of his injury and it was all he could do to put one foot in front of the other.

Tanya saw the difficulty he was in and slowed even more, but didn't stop. 'Just a few more minutes, Rudy. Remember the plan?'

'Uh huh.' Drake nodded without looking at her. They would enter the MU9 hangar and prep the two aircraft closest to the doors. Then, when all was ready and the only thing left to do was to release the spring, they would open the doors just enough for them to taxi out. Hopefully, by that time, even if someone saw the doors opening, they would be too far away to interfere before they had taken off.

The two of them had debated which machines to steal. Tanya had been all for stealing a couple of Blutsaugers, or even Gruber's machine, but she agreed that it was far too likely that a guard would be permanently posted within the Baron's hangar and was too big a risk. Drake had suggested an MU10 because they could both go in a single one, but in the end they had agreed to take a couple of MU9's because they were faster and would also be easier to prep on their own and quicker to get in the air.

Two hundred yards from the hangars they slowed to a walk, both so that Drake could get his breath back and so that they wouldn't make as much noise, in case someone was within and awake. There were no signs of life, though; no mechanic working late, no guard walking a beat. It seemed the Prussians were supremely confident that being so far behind the army lines made them safe and not for the first time did Drake wish that they could afford the time to disabuse them of that belief and do something to the aircraft, set them on fire or something, but they couldn't and he was just going to have to be satisfied with stealing two of them.

They were fifty yards from the first of the huge buildings when there was a brilliant flash of yellow light, like the sun had risen suddenly, and they were picked up off their feet and tossed aside by a hot wind.

Drake landed heavily and pain shot up his arm, but he was mildly surprised when it didn't snap again. He stared at the sky for a second while he made sure that he was in one piece, all of his limbs still present, before rolling onto his side and looking at the hangars, or what was left of them.

Three of them, the ones containing MU9's and MU10's, had collapsed in on themselves and were nothing more than heaps of twisted metal, but the fourth, the one that had contained the Baron aircraft had been blown completely apart by the force of the blast, peeled like an orange, and there was a fire raging in the remains. Luckily for the two escapees that hangar was the furthest from them and the others had absorbed some of the force of the blast.

Tanya was lying next to him and she pushed herself up on her elbows then groaned when she saw the wreckage. 'This is getting ridiculous.' She glanced at him. 'I'm starting to think that you're bad luck.'

'I'm starting to think the same.' He looked around. Lights were coming on everywhere and an alarm was sounding, almost drowning out the shouts of men streaming out of the buildings.

'Time to run, Rudy. We'll lose them in the forest, no problem.'

'Righty ho, one last crack at freedom, eh?'

They struggled to their feet and staggered woozily towards the trees, less than a hundred yards away, holding onto each other for support. Tanya stumbled and almost dragged Drake down with her, but somehow he managed to hold her up and they kept going. Finally they managed to get a good rhythm going between them, almost as if they were in a three-legged race, and he took the opportunity to glance over his shoulder.

Dozens of Prussians were charging across the airfield towards the hangars, but the pilots were off to one side of the blaze, in the relative darkness, and the men didn't seem to have seen them yet. It wouldn't take them long to do so, though, and their only hope was to get to the trees and into cover before they did.

When Drake had run the hundred yard dash at school, the races had been done almost in the blink of an eye, with barely enough time to take a breath, but it seemed to be taking them an eternity to cover the open ground. His back itched and he cringed as he ran, expecting the bullets to strike at any moment, but they never did and at last they were in among the trees.

Tanya pulled him to a halt and looked back. 'They're not following,'

'Even so, let's not push our luck by hanging around here, shall we?' He grinned, then reluctantly turned away from the spectacle of the devastated hangars.

Before he had even taken a step, he came face to face with a Prussian soldier who seemed to just materialise out of the darkness.

'Oh!' Drake wasn't sure who was more surprised, him or the Prussian, but Tanya certainly wasn't and she shoved him to the side and thrust her stolen knife into the man's throat.

Blood sprayed, hitting Drake in the eyes and he turned away in horror, wiping at his face with the sleeve of his greatcoat while trying to forget the look on the face of the young man, barely more than a youth, as he realised his life was at an end. However, when the shouts and screams began, he abandoned his efforts and blinked through the liquid.

The boy hadn't been alone. There were about a dozen more soldiers with him, or at least there had been, because three were already on the floor motionless, leaking red as Tanya spun through them like a whirlwind.

Drake watched her, mesmerised, for long seconds until finally realising that he should probably be helping her.

He had no training beyond his boxing and knew that was going to be completely ineffectual against the Prussians, but he threw himself into the fight anyway, figuring that if he could distract at least a couple of them then it would make Tanya's fight just that little bit easier.

He lasted less than five seconds.

Drake was a great proponent of the Marquess of Queensberry rules, but the Prussians quite obviously weren't and, while he was taking on one opponent and jabbing him satisfactorily on the nose, rocking him back on his heels, two more sneaked up on him in a most unsportsmanlike-fashion and bore him to the floor.

The last thing he saw before a rifle butt filled his vision was Tanya, screaming like a banshee, surrounded by more men than she could possibly handle, their guns pointed at her.

CHAPTER 11

'Guten Tag, Lord Drake. Are you hungry?'

Drake's eyes blinked open to find Hans Gruber sitting opposite him, the knife and fork in his hands poised over a large plate filled with sausage and vegetables, including cabbage.

'Huh? What?' His voice was barely audible, even to himself, over the racket the engines were making and he took a sip from the glass of water he found on the table in front of him.

Still drowsy and not quite sure why he wasn't lying dead in the snow of the Prussian airfield, he looked around.

If it hadn't already been obvious by the sound of the Fischer-Berg engines, the small windows, low rounded roof, and rows of deeply padded seats all confirmed that he was indeed aboard a Prussian aircraft.

He was facing the back of the machine, on one side of a large wooden table with four seats, which occupied almost the entire width of the craft, leaving just enough space for someone to pass. As far as he could see, there were no other conventional seats in the entire aircraft, just a couple of armchairs and a sofa, placed around a low coffee table, near to the rear bulkhead.

His vision swam suddenly and he put his head in his hands and stared down at the table, waiting for the dizzy spell to stop.

Gruber grinned. 'What you are feeling are the after-effects of the drug the doctors had to give you during treatment. The anti-aircraft crew who you came across were a little, how shall we say, *enthusiastic* in punishing you for the death of half their number and you required extensive surgery all last night and this morning to repair the damage. Among other things they broke your collarbone and left arm again and did something to your right knee that the doctors tried to explain to me, but I didn't understand.'

Drake lifted his head. 'An anti-aircraft crew... Damn, forgot about those blighters.' He remembered Gwen telling him about the numerous ack-ack and machine guns stationed in the woods, defending the airbase, which had taken such a toll among the unfortunate Muscovite bombers. Of course they would have sent troops to investigate the explosions.

He sat back in his seat and groaned as pain spiked through him from various parts of his body. Gruber hadn't been lying about his injuries - it felt like he'd been run over by a wagon. Several times.

'I rather imagined you had, otherwise you wouldn't have run straight into them.' Gruber laughed. 'Anyway, what I asked you was if you would like anything to eat.' He gestured at his food with his knife, even as he stuck a laden fork in his mouth. 'I'll have a plate prepared for you.'

Drake grimaced as particles of meat sprayed over the table, but no matter how much the man disgusted him, he wasn't going to say anything; he had to be at least moderately pleasant to the man until he was sure that Tanya was safe. He couldn't afford to be squeamish either; the rumbling of his stomach was telling him that he needed food.

'I'd like that, please.'

Gruber grunted and jerked his chin at someone Drake couldn't see at the front of the aircraft.

Drake tried to twist in his seat to look, but found that his wrists were bound to the arms of his seat. He raised an eyebrow at Gruber who grinned and shrugged.

'After you ripped apart half that crew and blew up the hangars, my guards insisted on you being restrained for my protection.'

'Guseva killed the soldiers, not me, and it wasn't us who blew up your hangars.'

'She is a ferocious young thing isn't she?' He laughed. 'And as for the hangars, I know it wasn't you and I don't really care.'

'What happened to Guseva? Was she killed?'

Drake prepared himself for the worst; he didn't think the Prussians would have let her live after she'd killed so many of them. He was relieved when Gruber shook his head.

'Everybody in this army knows better than to kill anyone in a red jumpsuit; it means you're mine. They hurt her badly, but she survived, don't worry.'

'Did the doctors take care of her as well?'

Gruber smirked. 'Let's just say she's in no immediate danger, but she's travelling in rather less comfort than we are, with the rest of my squadron.'

As if proving how well Gruber was treating his prisoner, a steward, the one from the pilot's mess, appeared from behind Drake. He laid a large plate of steaming food on the table, then used a cooking knife to slice through the ropes binding him. While he rubbed some life back into his wrists, Drake smiled his thanks at the man, who began to smile back, then seemed to remembered himself and nodded coolly at Gruber before hurrying off.

Drake could feel Gruber's eyes on him as he began tucking in, but, even though he was exceedingly hungry, he wasn't going to give the man the satisfaction of seeing him slip, so he kept his manners perfect while still eating as quickly as he could.

After several mouthfuls, he felt more himself and he wiped his mouth, then looked up at Gruber, curious. 'You don't look at all upset that your aircraft were destroyed.'

'I'm not.'

'Shouldn't you be? I mean, aren't your superiors going to be a little disappointed that you're abandoning the northern front?'

'Not at all.' Gruber shook his head, but Drake thought he saw a hint of doubt in the man's eyes when they flickered to the black Prussian eagle, emblazoned on the red velvet headrests of the seats. 'On the contrary, while the destruction of the aircraft is only a temporary setback for which I am not to blame, my destruction of Wasp is a propaganda coup, showing the continuing weakness of the Misfits and their female pilots. I consider my job in the north done and now I'm going to head south for the winter, like the aerial creature I am; there is much more important work for me in Italy and I already have plenty of aircraft to replace the ones that were lost.'

'Italy? That's nice. It'll be good to get some sunshine.'

Gruber chuckled, shaking his head. 'I'm afraid you won't get much sun where you're going.'

'And where is that?'

'You'll see.'

Gruber smiled enigmatically, but said nothing more as he turned his full attention to the remains of his meal and Drake was glad to do the same.

A change in the engine note brought Drake out of a deep sleep and he sat up and looked around with bleary eyes.

He had become increasingly drowsy as he'd eaten and wasn't sure if he'd finished before succumbing to exhaustion.

'Maybe I should have warned you that there were sedatives and painkillers in your water. Oops.' Gruber appeared from behind Drake, grinning widely as he sat in his seat and did his safety belt up. His day uniform had been replaced by the smart black dress uniform and his hair was slicked back severely.

Drake wasn't amused. 'That would have been decent of you, yes.'

The Prussian laughed and spread his arms wide. 'But then I would have been deprived of the sight of you dive bombing your plate!'

'I'm glad I was able to provide some amusement for you, even unconsciously.' He reached up to touch his face, searching for traces of the food but there weren't any.

'Don't worry, I had the steward clean you up; I'm not a complete barbarian.' Gruber saw Drake's sour expression and pouted. 'Oh, come on, you were a university man - surely you played pranks on your fellow students? I know I did.'

Drake sighed. 'Yes. But they were my friends.'

'Well, I still believe we could be friends.'

Drake blinked in surprise, temporarily lost for words; it was the second time the man had brought up the subject of friendship. He wondered what motive he could have for doing so, whether he genuinely believed it or if it were some kind of crude attempt at manipulation. He eventually managed to force a smile. 'As I said before, it's possible.'

'Of course it is! Just look at us - a British Lord and a movie star, both highly decorated fighter pilots.' Gruber laughed. 'It would make a wonderful flyvie. Perhaps I will have someone start on the script!'

'Well, don't expect me to play myself.'

'Why not? I think you would be a good actor. You have the looks for it and the women would be clambering over each other to get their hands on you.'

Drake shook his head. 'That kind of thing is not important to me.'

'Again I ask, why not?' Gruber seemed genuinely puzzled, but then his face lit up with understanding. 'Ah, you have one special woman in mind. Officer Stone, ya?' He grinned suddenly. 'Or is it Praporshik Guseva who now holds your heart?'

'Under my current circumstances, I don't think that really matters, do you?'

'Indeed not!'

While they had been talking, the aircraft had been steadily descending and now there were a series of dull thumps as the undercarriage descended and locked into place.

Gruber gave Drake a last smile, then turned to peer out of the window. 'Ah, here we are at last. While we refuel, I will be making my report at the War Office. You will wait with the aircraft.'

Drake wondered at the nervous note that had crept into the man's voice, but it and the curious conversation were forgotten when he followed the Prussian's gaze.

The empty blue through the window next to him had given way to the greens and greys of the buildings and parks of a sprawling city and Drake started when he recognised some of the architecture. They were the monstrous, narcissistic edifices that had been put up in the Prussian capital since Kaiser Wilhelm III came to power.

Gruber had brought him to Berlin.

In the thirties, the Kaiser had announced to the world his intention of making Prussia, and Berlin in particular, the cultural centre of the world, like Athens and Rome had been in their time. The buildings, emulating the grand edifices of those cities, were the first stage of that plan.

His ambition had been applauded by many until, years later, he announced the second stage of his grand plan - to make the city the *actual* centre of the world by *conquering* the rest of it.

Tempelhof airport appeared beneath them and the aircraft settled gently to the concrete runway, braking equally gently as it made the long run towards the huge terminal, itself one of those new buildings, before finally coming to a halt under the overhang.

Gruber had unbuckled himself and was out of his seat almost as soon as the aircraft had landed, but Drake didn't trust his legs or balance and waited until it had come to a full stop and the engines were powering down before standing. By the time he'd hobbled to the rear of the aircraft, Gruber was already down the steps and standing on the tarmac, staring at a large black autocar flying twin Prussian flags. It didn't seem to be what he had been expecting, though.

The anxiety Drake had thought he'd detected earlier was now plain to see and he struggled to keep his face straight. 'Everything alright, old chap?'

'Yes, fine, of course. Why wouldn't it be?' Gruber replied distractedly, without taking his eyes from the vehicle.

It seemed the man wasn't so sure of his welcome after all and his doubts had only been exacerbated by the appearance of an Imperial autocar, instead of the ministry one that he'd expected. Drake was sorely tempted to comment further and feed those fears, so as to take a small measure of revenge, but managed to restrain himself.

A soldier stepped out of the autocar and marched smartly over. He saluted Gruber. 'The Kaiser requests your presence at the palace, sir.'

Gruber returned the salute with a nod, then turned to Drake. 'Looks like I might be a bit longer than I thought. Try not to get yourself into trouble.' He laughed as he strutted across the tarmac, but it sounded false and by the time he got into the autocar all traces of his good humour had gone, replaced by a worried frown.

Drake watched the black machine power away across the apron, then turned in place, looking around curiously.

Tempelhof airport hadn't changed much since he'd flown over to Berlin with his Prussian girlfriend during the summer hols in 1937. The immense quarter circle of the terminal building, fully three quarters of a mile wide, was the same and so was the huge concrete apron, but it had completely lost its previous welcoming aspect, in favour of something far more martial and forbidding. The multitudes of passengers were all gone, as were the colourful advertisements for everything from whisky to underwear and the signs showing the locations of the offices of the airline companies. In their place, hanging from almost every available surface, was the Prussian flag, which had been recently modernised to strike fear into the enemy wherever the invincible Prussian army went - the black eagle had been stylised, made harsher, and now appeared on a new background of a white circle on a blood red field.

It was all very intimidating, but Drake wondered who the effort was being made for, because there weren't many aircraft in evidence. Unlike Hyde airstrip, where grounded civilian aircraft were littered everywhere, here there were just a few transport aircraft and a single squadron of sixteen sleek, red-nosed MU9's lined up neatly near the end of the runway, most likely the Prussian equivalent of the Royal Guard squadron.

A whirring sound and a honk from behind him made Drake jump and he limped painfully to one side as two spring-powered gas bowsers trundled up to the aircraft, silent on their rubber tyres. He shook his head at the sight; where before the large tankers had been brightly painted with the insignias of the airlines to which they belonged, now they were a dull grey and emblazoned with the new Prussian flag.

Drake laughed as a sudden image came to him. He had a cousin, several years younger than him, who had been gifted with a rubber name stamp for her third birthday so that she could "sign" her name on the family letters and cards. Instead, for weeks afterwards, she had used it to stamp everything in sight, including unfortunate pets, declaring "mine" each time.

Unfortunately, the Prussians were putting their stamp on other countries in a very permanent manner, with no parents to tell them differently.

He idly watched the attendants hook the bowsers up to the tanks in the wings of the aircraft and begin the refuelling process, but then his attention was drawn by the drone of approaching engines and he shaded his eyes and scanned the horizon.

He quickly found the aircraft on final approach. It was a transport, similar to the one that he and Gruber had flown in, but while theirs was a sleek luxury model, shiny and new, with upgraded engines, this was very much a workhorse and shabby from use.

The aircraft landed with a screech and a puff of burnt rubber then taxied over, coming to rest less than thirty yards away. It disgorged the rest of the Crimson Baron pilots, who glanced nervously in the direction of Gruber's aircraft, but when they saw Drake on his own they seemed to relax and a couple wandered off to the terminal building, while the rest wandered around, stretching their legs and backs.

Drake eyed the other transport. Gruber had said that Tanya was travelling with the other pilots. There was no sign of her, though, and he decided to stroll over and ask them about her, thinking that they'd be more likely to open up to him without their commander there. However, as soon as he made a move in their direction, the soldier who'd been set to watch him lifted his machine gun in warning and shook his head.

Drake smiled and backed off, raising his hands, even as he silently cursed the man's stubborn devotion to duty, after all, where did he think he was going to go in the middle of Berlin? He went and sat on the stairs of Gruber's aircraft, conveniently facing the older transport, hoping that he'd catch a glimpse of the Muscovite.

The pilots who'd gone off soon returned with magazines which they passed out and the men spent the rest of the time while their aircraft was being refuelled laughing about the articles in them. Every so often one of them would glance towards Drake, but none of them ever made any move to speak to him.

Finally, the bowsers finished their work on both machines and the pilots stood and went back onboard their aircraft, grumbling good-naturedly. Drake gave up all hope of seeing Tanya when the engines coughed into life, but then, right before they sealed the hatch, one of the pilots reappeared in the opening, looked in his direction and subtly tilted his head towards the front of the aircraft.

Eagerly, Drake scanned the forward windows of the transport and a few seconds later a face appeared at the one closest to the nose. He didn't recognise her at first because her face was swollen and blackened, but then her mouth cracked into the smile he'd grown to know so well over the past week. She waved, both hands coming up to do so, showing him that she was bound, but then she was jerked away and a guard appeared in her place. He peered out, saw Drake, his hand still raised in greeting, and scowled before disappearing again.

As the other aircraft taxied away, Drake leaned back against the steps. Even though Tanya was obviously not being transported in the same style as he was and her injuries had once again been treated only in a perfunctory fashion, she didn't seem too much the worse for wear.

With his fears about her assuaged, he got himself as comfortable as he could in the weak German sunlight, which felt decidedly warm after the far northern weather he'd become accustomed to, and allowed himself to drift off.

The sun was going down when the steward shook him gently awake by the shoulder.

'Sir?'

Drake blinked up at the man. 'Yes?'

'We've just received word that the Generalleutnant will not be returning tonight. His orders are for you to stay on board. I've prepared you a dinner and I will make you up a bed on the sofa, if that is acceptable?'

'Perfectly, thank you.'

Drake groaned at his the aches in his muscles, made much worse by sleeping too long with the steps digging into his back and followed him into the aircraft.

The steward had whipped him up toad in the hole with onion gravy and vegetables and there was half a bottle of French red wine to wash it down. That was followed by spotted dick and custard. It was all very British fare, very unlike what had been on offer until then, and it was obvious that the steward was taking advantage of Gruber's not being there to prepare something to his guest's taste rather than his master's.

Drake also took advantage of his host's absence to properly enjoy the food. He also had the chance to properly look at the steward for the first time - one aspect of the manners drummed into him by his mother was that it was not done to notice the help too much, something he heartily disagreed with.

The man was in his early fifties and thin, with greying dark brown hair parted in the middle. Despite his carefully schooled impassive expression he looked exhausted, something that didn't surprise Drake; having to take care of the child-like Gruber had to be extremely tiring. However, there was also a hint of sorrow in his brown eyes that was slightly puzzling.

While he was eating, he tried to engage the man in conversation, but he just nodded and gave a meaningful look at the two guards standing at the forward bulkhead, watching his every move, so he had to settle for merely smiling his thanks. It wasn't until the meal was cleared away and the steward was making Drake's bed on the sofa for the night that he had a chance to speak.

'Do you speak English?'

The steward swivelled to grab a blanket from an armchair, using the motion to snatch a look at the guards. They were at the other end of the aircraft still, out of earshot, but easily able to see them talking and would be sure to report everything they saw to Gruber. He turned back and continued with his task. 'Yes, sir, but we shouldn't.'

'I know, but I want to thank you. For everything.'

'There is no need, sir, I merely did what I felt was right.'

The man turned away to pick up the pillows that had been with the blankets and Drake shot a glance at the guards. They were relaxed, talking and barely glancing in his direction, but even so, it would be best not to push his luck with an extended conversation; he didn't want to do anything that would possibly get the steward into hot water.

'What is your name?'

'Friedrich, sir, Friedrich Lang.'

'My friends call me Rudy and I hope some day you'll be able to do so without it getting you in trouble.'

'I'd like that, my Lord.' The steward gave a slight smile, then gestured at the bed. 'All ready, sir. Goodnight.'

'Goodnight, Friedrich.'

A guard kicked Drake rudely awake just after dawn, but it wasn't until late midmorning that the black autocar returned.

He half-hoped that whatever Gruber had been worried about had come to pass and he'd been retained for some kind of dressing-down, but the man was all smiles despite his obvious tiredness when he clambered out and there was a definite bounce in his step as he sauntered over to the aircraft and mounted the stairs. His voice was just as harsh as ever when he shouted at nobody in particular for them to take off, though, and he didn't even glance in Drake's direction as he took his seat, calling for champagne.

Gruber stayed silent, sipping his drink and gazing out of the window, the smile still on his face, as the aircraft took off, but as soon as it levelled out he stood and went to the back of the aircraft where there was a bedroom that Drake hadn't been permitted to use. He came back ten minutes later wearing his day uniform and tossed a red velvet box, like the ones that necklaces came in, on the table in front of Drake before flopping bonelessly into his seat.

Drake looked at him inquisitively, but the man just waved at the box, so he opened it.

Inside was a thick black ribbon with a large gold medal attached to it. Picked out in black stone on the medal was a Prussian cross. It was impressive, but at the same time stark and severe and typically Prussian.

Gruber grinned. 'My reward for shooting down Wasp. I am now a member of the "Teutonic Order of the Prussian Empire", which gives me direct access to the Emperor, a stipend that is far more than I get as an actor and lands in Bavaria.'

Drake snapped the box closed and slid it back across the table to him. 'Congratulations.'

'Thank you.' Gruber took the box and placed it on the seat beside him, then reclined his chair and closed his eyes. He was snoring in seconds, competing with the engines for volume.

Drake stared at him for long seconds, worrying at the contradictions within the man. Gruber was like a child; all smiles one minute, then throwing a tantrum the next and he wasn't sure if he was looking forward to the day when he decided that Drake wasn't a toy he wanted to play with anymore and decided to discard him.

CHAPTER 12

A few hours from Berlin, just after lunch, the aircraft began steadily gaining height. At first Drake thought they were just climbing to cross the Alps into Italy, but when they kept going up, well beyond what was necessary, he realised that something else was going on. He would have looked to Gruber for answers, but the man was still sleeping, curled up in his fully reclined seat and drooling onto the Prussian crest on the headrest. Instead he looked around for the steward, Friedrich, wondering if he would dare to answer a question or two now that Gruber was back.

The man came forward at his glance and gave a small bow. He was back to his cool impassiveness now that Gruber had returned. 'Yes, sir? Would you like something? Some tea perhaps? There is also some fresh bread - I could make you a bacon sandwich.'

He hadn't remarked it the previous night, but the man's English was surprisingly good, with a refined accent, and he wondered if the man had been a servant in one of the grand Prussian houses before Gruber had gotten his grubby hands on him. He gave him a wide smile. 'That sounds wonderful, thank you, but first, do you know why we're climbing so high?'

The steward gave Gruber a nervous glance, then leaned to speak into Drake's ear. 'We are almost at Bertha, sir.'

Without giving any further explanation, the man turned on his heel.

Bertha? Surely he'd misheard over the sound of the straining engines, but if he hadn't, who or what was Bertha?

He didn't have long to wait because, almost as soon as he'd finished his sandwich and tea, the steward returned and bent over Gruber to shake him gently awake. 'We're on final approach, sir.'

Gruber just grunted in return and allowed the man to help him put his seat upright. He wiped his mouth with the back of his sleeve before smiling at Drake. 'Let's go take a look, shall we?'

Gruber motioned for Drake to follow him and led the way forward to the cockpit. The two men flying the aircraft looked around in surprise as they went through the door, but quickly returned their attention to their jobs - the pilot continuing a call with someone, while the copilot kept an eye on a small instrument on the panel in front of him that Drake didn't recognise.

Gruber bent over the pilot to peer through the windscreen and Drake did the same. A glance at the altimeter showed him that they were almost at twelve thousand metres, something like forty thousand feet, and he frowned; this high there was nothing at all to see apart from the bright blue sky. They were even far above the clouds. 'What am I supposed to be looking at?'

Gruber glanced at the unfamiliar instrument on the panel. 'We're still quite far away, but you'll see soon enough.'

He patted the pilot on the shoulder and when the man looked up at him he jerked his thumb over his shoulder. 'Out,' he said in German. 'I'll take us in.'

'Yes, sir.'

The pilot nervously fumbled with the quick release catch at his navel, then hurriedly stood, surrendering his seat to Gruber. The Prussian didn't bother strapping himself in before trying the controls to get the feel of the aircraft, making it dip and weave gently. Once he was satisfied he glanced over his shoulder at Drake. 'Why don't you take the copilot's controls?'

Even though Gruber hadn't said anything directly to him, the copilot couldn't get out of the cockpit fast enough.

Drake took his seat and did up the safety straps to Gruber's amusement.

'Don't you trust me to get us down safely?'

'I don't trust anyone behind a stick except myself.'

'Not even Gwen Stone?'

Drake avoided the question by tapping the unknown instrument with a fingertip. It comprised of two round electronic screens, side by side, a jagged and jumping waveform with a single spike on each. 'What's this for?'

'That's a radio direction finder. It shows us where Bertha is.'

'She must be a very elusive woman if you need a tracking device to find her. What is she, your girlfriend?'

Gruber laughed. 'She's the closest thing I have to one and yes, she is *extremely* elusive. The best-kept secret in the world in fact.'

Drake waited, but when it was obvious the man wasn't going to be any more forthcoming he gestured at the instrument. 'How do I use this then?'

'The screen on the left is direction, the one on the right is altitude. If the spikes are in the middle we're on the correct course at the correct height. The closer we get to Bertha, the higher the spikes get, and when they reach the top of the display we're there.'

Drake nodded. 'Sounds easy enough.'

Gruber chuckled again. 'I know! But apparently it takes three days to train our men to use it.' He jerked his chin at the instrument. 'Tell me what our status is.'

Drake peered at it, taking in the graduations along the x and y axes of the screens. 'I'm assuming this is calibrated in metres...' He looked sideways at Gruber, but when he didn't reply he continued. 'In which case we are on course, five hundred metres below and approximately ten kilometres from our target.'

Gruber gave the instrument a quick glance. 'Looks about right, well done.'

As the waveforms crept higher and higher Drake looked from the instruments to the sky outside to Gruber, but the man said nothing, nor could he see anything.

It wasn't until they had closed to less than five kilometres that Gruber finally turned to him and grinned. 'There she is - Bertha, the *Bertha Berg*, named after the mother in law of the man who conceived of her.'

Drake leaned forward to squint through the windscreen. 'I don't...'

A flash of sunlight on metal drew his eye and he fell silent, his mouth going dry, as he finally saw their destination.

Bertha was painted a light blue that almost matched the sky, which was why it had taken so long for him to make her out.

She was the biggest airborne craft he had ever seen.

Five gigantic Zeppelin hulls had been needed to bear aloft an immense gondola, roughly the same shape as the Arturo, with angular sides, a vertical stern and a sharp prow, but far larger. Four immense fans protruded from the corners of her flat keel and were powering it along at a fair clip, but curiously there were no engines in evidence or any exhaust fumes to be seen.

The paintwork really did a remarkable job of camouflaging the aircraft and Drake could see how Gruber could claim that it was the best-kept secret in the world. Even the iron cross insignia of the Fliegertruppe, usually black, were merely outlines, picked out on the fins and sides in white, so as not to spoil the effect.

'Bertha took three years to build at a top secret facility on the Rhine, near the Swiss border. She is almost six hundred metres long and just under five hundred wide, made almost entirely of Duralumin, and has a crew of five hundred. She never has to land and she hasn't since she was launched - anything she needs is ferried to her by aircraft.'

There was a note of real pride in Gruber's voice as he spoke about the airship which Drake could well understand; Bertha was an unparalleled feat of engineering and undoubtedly unique in the world.

'How is she powered?'

'Wind turbines generate electricity for the entire ship and the fans are run by the largest springs ever designed.'

Drake frowned. 'But how do you wind them? Surely if you need steam engines to wind the springs you might as well just have those engines powering the fans.'

Gruber grinned at him. 'Don't worry; you'll see for yourself soon enough.'

The Prussian swung them in a wide arc around the gondola to approach from the rear and for a moment Drake thought that they were going to land on top of it, as if it were an aircraft carrier, but then a bright line appeared near the top of the stern as an enormous hangar door opened, moving downwards. Drake winced as he saw it, thinking that it would take a piece of impressive piloting to get them inside safely, but he had misjudged the proportions and, as they neared it on final approach, he realised that the gap was far bigger than he'd thought. The landing deck inside Bertha was larger than some airfields that Drake had seen in fact, large enough to double as the hangar deck, and it was so long that there was no need for arrester hooks to stop the aircraft. Gruber didn't even have to apply the brakes very hard; he merely kept rolling until he'd passed the line of aircraft parked beside the runway, including the transport that had been carrying Tanya and five Blutsaugers, before bringing the transport to a halt. He ignored the signals of a man trying to direct them to their parking place and stood, leaving the engines running. 'Let's leave this for the pilot to take care of.'

He led Drake to the still-sealed door at the rear of the aircraft where the steward was waiting for them. He had an oxygen mask in place over his face and was holding two more, along with their greatcoats.

Gruber shrugged into his long black coat and put on his mask, then waited impatiently for Drake to do the same.

Drake was glad to do so; the temperature had been dropping for a while and the air was becoming decidedly thin.

Gruber saw his discomfort and grinned through the glass faceplate of the mask. 'We've been equalising pressure for the last couple of minutes. Unless you want to suffocate, I'd get that mask on quickly.'

Drake put on his coat, then pulled the mask on hurriedly. It had a hose attached to a small backpack which went over his shoulders. The steward showed him the controls, switching it on so that there was a steady flow of air, then turned to the outer door and waited, his eyes on a red light over the door. When it went green he turned the handle.

There was barely a hiss as the door opened and as soon as the steward had the steps in place Gruber bounced down them to the metal floor of the cavernous space.

A long line of men, standing smartly at attention, was waiting for them on the flight deck. Gruber's pilots in their grey *Fliegertruppe* uniforms were at one end and there were a few soldiers of *Die Reichsheer*, the Prussian Imperial Army, in green, but the rest, the vast majority, were sailors wearing dark blue - it seemed that an airship fell under the purview of the Prussian Imperial Navy, *Die Reichsflotte*, rather than the air force. The leader of the men, a painfully thin man with receding grey hair in a blue uniform dripping with gold, saluted, and for once Gruber returned the gesture properly and with respect.

'Welcome back, Generalleutnant.'

'Thank you, Admiral. How is the ship?'

While Gruber conversed with the naval officer, Drake took in his surroundings with interest.

Aside from the two transports and shiny new Blutsaugers, on which mechanics were still stencilling names and victory markings, there were two large cargo aircraft in the hangar, one of which was being unloaded by a line of soldiers in green army uniforms and the other preparing for takeoff. White lines on the otherwise unpainted metal floor marked the limits of the runway and taxiways and there were boxes sitting at regular intervals, showing where aircraft were meant to park, red ones for the Baron fighters and yellow ones for the larger aircraft.

Even as vast as it was, the hangar didn't take up the entire deck and there were wide bulkhead doors leading off both flanks, the closest of which was open, giving him a view of workshop where a Blutsauger was under construction.

It was all extremely impressive, but what struck him most was the quiet. While there was obviously a fair amount of noise from the people and aircraft, there was no deep thrum from the engines like there had been on the Arturo and no ever-present vibration in the deck. If it weren't for the masks that everyone was wearing, they could almost be on solid ground and the fact that he knew they weren't just added to the sense of awe the giant airship had provoked in him.

He turned at a clang and saw that the hangar door they had come through had just closed. There was a loud hissing noise from all around and then less than half a minute later a klaxon sounded that had everyone removing their masks. Drake did the same and tested the air - it was dry and thin, like the air at about ten thousand feet, and there was a metallic smell to it, but it was perfectly breathable. He shook his head in wonder; he'd heard of scientists working on pressurising the cockpits of aircraft to remove the need for oxygen masks, but this was the technology taken to a whole other scale.

He was starting to feel rather dismayed; the more he learnt of the airship, the more he realised that the British were not only out-gunned and out-manned, but also lagging far behind when it came to the technology of war. He chuckled wryly to himself; just as well they made up for the deficit with good, old-fashioned pluck, stiff upper lip and brilliant pilots.

Friedrich, the steward, appeared as if from nowhere. He murmured an apology and took Drake's breathing apparatus from him, disappearing into the aircraft with it. Drake wondered why the man had apologised, but then noticed that he was now the only person without one. Evidently he wasn't going to need one wherever he was going - he just hoped they weren't planning on opening the hangar doors again before he got there.

Shortly after, Gruber finished his conversation with the admiral and beckoned Drake over.

'I'm afraid I have urgent business to attend to, but when that is concluded I'll take you on a tour of the ship.'

He waved forward the guards from the transport and spoke to them in German. 'Take him to station three.' He glanced at the admiral with a smirk. 'Let's see if he's still as confident and aristocratic after some time at the capstans.'

The admiral nodded then looked at Drake, giving him what on the surface was a polite and respectful nod. 'Welcome aboard, Lord Drake. I hope you have a pleasant stay on board.'

'Thank you, Admiral.' Drake returned the nod, not betraying the fact that he had understood what Gruber had said or that he was worried about what he meant; capstans were used to raise anchors on sailing ships, but the airship couldn't possibly need such a thing.

He hoped that his rusty German had provided an incorrect translation because the alternative, that it was a name they were putting to some kind of torture device, wasn't one that he particularly wanted to contemplate.

CHAPTER 13

The guards took him through a thick door in the middle of the hangar and into a small connecting room, about five yards square, which was labelled "Pressure Chamber" in German. It was bare apart from a second door opposite the first, control panels by both doors and a few metal cabinets lining a wall to his right. As they went past the cabinets, Drake read the labels on them and found that they contained emergency supplies - breathing masks, firefighting equipment and, of all things, glidewings.

The door on the far side of the room took them directly into a stairwell, like the one in the Arturo which had gone from the depths of the ship all the way up to the hangar deck, and they started down.

Large blue numbers were painted on the walls next to the bulkhead doors on each floor, with what was on each of them stencilled in white underneath. As they descended and the numbers increased (the hangar had been on deck three), Drake read the words with interest, noting, among other things, that the pilots' mess was on deck four and there were two decks, five and six, solely dedicated to accommodation. However, despite the marvellous work of the Prussian doctors, his knee was aching and his legs were shaking with exhaustion by the time they reached deck nine and he barely had the energy to lift his head from the floor to read "Navy Officers' Mess".

He stopped to catch his breath and leaned over the banister to look down, goggling when he saw that they were only slightly more than half way down. 'Bloody hell isn't there a lift?'

The guards shoved him back into movement, but they did it without rancour and just continued chatting, seemingly not at all worried about Drake trying to escape and he realised that, even if he did somehow manage to get away from them, he had absolutely nowhere to go. Stealing an aircraft was out of the question this time with no idea how to open the hangar doors.

Black spots were swimming in front of his eyes by the time they reached the correct floor, only a couple of flights from the bottom. There were white words on the wall next to the door under the large blue eighteen, but he didn't have a chance to read them before the guards took him through and into a bare metal corridor that was so long that he couldn't see the end of it. The corridor was empty at least as far as he could tell, except for two doors, about ten yards in, facing each other, one painted with a big red "4" and the other a "3".

Behind door number 3 was a large guard room. It had bare metal walls like the corridor outside, but was comfortably appointed with a dining table that seated eight, a few sofas, and a bookshelf stuffed with books and magazines. A doorway to the side lead to an adjoining room which had beds in it and the sound of running water hinted at a shower somewhere nearby. The corridors and the stairwell had been cold and unheated, but here there was warm air coming out of an overhead vent, making the room wonderfully cosy.

'Got another one for you.'

Three men in naval uniforms were playing cards at the table and they looked up at the soldier's call. One of them threw down his cards and got to his feet, joking with the others about not looking, then led Drake and the guards over to a door at the back of the room, unclipping a bunch of keys from his belt as he went.

While he was waiting for the sailor to undo the locks, Drake amused himself with reading the signs on the control panel on the wall next to the door. It had controls and gauges for things like lights, heat, air and pressure, and at the bottom was a large red lever marked "release" with a keyhole next to it.

The sailor got the door open and he ushered Drake and his guards inside a pressure room like the one they had passed through to leave the hangar, complete with the same emergency supplies. When they were inside he closed the door, then moved across to another identical door and repeated the unlocking process. There were no controls here to occupy Drake's attention so he just watched the man as he turned two large keys, spun a metal wheel, identical to the ones on the heavier bulkhead doors of the Arturo, then tugged on the door to swing it open.

At the guards' prompting, Drake followed the man through onto a small balcony, which was already occupied by another couple of sailors, and stumbled to a halt.

Ten yards below, in a room that was fully fifty yards square, more than a hundred men and women in red jumpsuits were pushing on poles that radiated like spokes from a giant metal cylinder, much like a capstan on a ship. They were dishevelled and ragged, their jumpsuits in varying degrees of grubbiness and disrepair, their hair and exposed skin filthy, the men invariably bearded. However, more than their appearance, it was the demeanour of the captives which shocked and disturbed Drake; barely anybody looked up at him as he leaned over the balcony and those that did, did so without much interest, their eyes empty.

The room stank, but not just of unwashed bodies and confined humanity - it stank of despair and of hopelessness.

He searched the sea of red for Tanya, hoping that she'd been sent to the same room as he, but the guards only allowed him a few seconds to stare at the scene below, as if to let the reality of his new circumstances sink in, before they pushed him to the side and down the stairs leading to the floor.

Two more sailors were on duty down below. They weren't armed with guns, but instead wielded rattan canes. One of them greeted the soldiers with a laugh before leering at Drake, and pointed at one of the capstan bars with his cane. The soldiers shoved Drake into position, stripped him of his greatcoat, then left quickly, obviously not wanting to be there any longer than they had to.

Drake placed his hands on the thick wooden bar, but he still couldn't quite believe that they were actually going to make him do it. The rules for the treatment of prisoners of war, set down by the third Geneva Convention, of which both Prussia and Britain had been signatories, forbade the compelling of officers to work. Quite apart from that, the Convention also made it very clear that no work was to be undertaken that was hazardous to the health of prisoners, regardless of their rank, yet here around him was evidence to the contrary in haggard faces and worn bodies.

It took a sharp rap on the arse from the sailor's cane to spur him into action and he glared at the grinning sailor, but nonetheless leant his strength to the efforts of the men and women around him. He seethed inside, not so much from the pain - he'd had much worse from the headmaster at Eton - but rather from the indignity and illegality of the treatment.

It didn't take him long to forget all about that, though, as his weakened condition soon had him once again fighting for breath and his world shrank to the wooden bar, the metal deck below and the effort of putting one foot in front of the other.

The task went on and on, the people trudging round in an endless circle. The only relief coming when positions at the bars were switched around, the men and women on the very inside changing to the outside and everyone else shuffling inwards, all without stopping.

The sailors guarding them only interjected a few times, mostly to "encourage" those who they considered weren't doing their utmost, but once they had to drag away a woman who had collapsed from exhaustion. Even though Drake wasn't doing much more than leaning on the bar, they ignored him, but whether that was because he was on his last legs and they knew it wouldn't have any effect, or they were under orders not to hurt him, he couldn't tell.

It seemed like hours later when a klaxon sounded. Almost as one, the entire crowd of people groaned and the capstan ground to a halt as they stopped pushing. Some staggered off, going towards a doorway opposite the entrance, but most just collapsed to the floor where they were.

It hadn't been particularly hard work - the force needed to push the bar round about the same as, say, pushing a drinks trolley - but after hours it had become back-breaking and Drake could only guess at the number of miles the prisoners walked each day.

He uncurled his cramped hands from the bar and let his legs go beneath him, fully intending to just drop where he fell, when arms went around him and helped him to sit far more gently than he would have. He leaned back against the cold metal of the central cylinder, then looked up to find Tanya smiling down at him.

'Hello Rudy. You look awful.'

'You don't look too hot yourself.' Her face was one solid bruise, her lips puffy and cracked, and her gums were once again a bloody mess - it was hard to imagine he looked worse. He was relieved to see that he wouldn't have to pay for any more gold teeth, though.

He tried to ask her how she was feeling, but a sudden wave of nausea hit him and he squeezed his eyes shut and gulped down deep breaths of the fetid air, trying to prevent himself from losing his lunch.

Once the dizzy spell had passed he looked up at her again, but before he could ask how she was feeling, a man in a tattered jumpsuit, so soiled that it could barely be described as red anymore, entered his field of vision and bent down to peer at him.

'Ace, old bean? Is that you?'

The man looked nothing less than a tramp - he was gaunt, with sunken eyes in a heavily lined, dirt-ingrained face, almost hidden behind long, filthy hair, and an equally long and filthy, scraggly beard. The voice was familiar, though, and Drake frowned up at the man, trying to place him. The use of the nickname he'd earned in France was a bit of a hint (he'd been given it jokingly when he'd become the first British "ace" of the war and only his first squadron had ever called him it), but it was the man's direct, penetrating stare, despite heavily bloodshot eyes, which finally gave him a clue as to the man's identity. 'Squadron Leader Askwith?'

'One and the same.' The man smiled, revealing rotting teeth and far too many gaps.

'Sir! We thought you were dead!'

'I might as well be, for all the good I'm doing in here.'

'We weren't informed you'd been captured, sir, so...'

Askwith had been the commander of Drake's squadron in France. In his forties, a veteran of the First Great War, he was one of many so-called "Flynosaurs" who'd been brought back from retirement to lend their experience to the new generation of pilots. He had gone missing in June, six months before, after a sortie over Prussian-held territory. No word had come from the Prussian army that he had been captured and they had naturally assumed the worst.

Askwith sighed and sat down. He groaned as he stretched his legs out in front of him and rubbed a calf as he spoke. 'I was afraid you'd say that. My wife must be worried sick.' He smiled wryly. 'Although, I guess I shouldn't be too surprised; as you can see, our hosts aren't exactly playing by the rules.' He made an expansive gesture. 'Welcome to the most secure prison camp in the Prussian Empire. Get nice and comfy because nobody has ever escaped.'

'How do you know?'

'Well, have you ever heard of this thing?'

'No.'

'Neither had I until I got here and I think if anyone had got out, they'd damn well have made sure to tell someone, wouldn't they?'

'Yes, they would.' Drake sighed. He knew that the man was right and any hope he was holding out for being able to escape, that Tanya might pull off a miracle, completely evaporated - it looked like his war was over and he was going to be forced to aid Gruber, of all people, in his war against the Misfits.

At the thought of the Muscovite, he belatedly realised that he'd been remiss in his manners and decided to rectify the situation. 'Uh, have you met Praporshik Guseva, sir?'

'We ask all new arrivals to tell us what's going on outside, so I heard her speak last night, but we haven't been formally introduced.' Askwith held out his hand. 'Squadron Leader Edward Arthur Askwith at your service, ma'am.'

Tanya took his hand. 'Tatiana Guseva, but you can call me Tanya.'

'Then you must call me Ted.'

Drake pouted. 'How come he gets to call you Tanya right away? I had to give you some of my rations before you let me do that.'

'Because I didn't trust you.' She pointed a finger at his face and twirled it in front of him. 'You have that look in your eyes, the one that says you are too used to having your way with women.'

'She's got you there, Ace!' Askwith chimed in.

'No she hasn't!'

Askwith smirked. 'Do I really have to remind you about that girl you sneaked off base to meet every night while we were training in Scotland? Or that young governess in Brighton while we were on leave? Or the Comte's daughter in Nancy? Or...'

When Askwith made to keep going with his list of Drake's many dalliances, he waved him to a stop desperately, looking shamefully at Tanya. 'Alright, alright, that's enough!'

As his two friends laughed at his discomfort, Drake sulked, crossing his arms and pointedly looking away from them to gaze around the room.

The woman who had been dragged away from the capstan had been left where she lay. There were a couple of men bent over her, trying to help, but she wasn't moving. Most of the others who'd dropped where they were had since picked themselves up and drifted towards the door, but some hadn't moved since the klaxon and didn't look like they intended to any time soon. He grimaced as he took in their grey complexions and emaciated features; that was most likely what awaited him in the weeks, months, or even years ahead.

When he finally tore his eyes away from the horrible scene, he found Tanya looking at him. 'This is not over, Rudy.' She reached out and squeezed his hand, giving him a smile, then turned away. Her eyes began darting around the room, taking it all in, following the guards as they chatted in a group near the stairs.

Drake smiled; it looked like she was already working on a way to get them out. Feeling better than he had since he'd been put to work, he turned back to Askwith. 'So, who are these people? Are they really all pilots?'

'As far as I know.' Askwith said. 'We've got representatives of most of the countries the Prussians have rolled over in the last year or so in here. There's Poles, French, Danes, Norwegians, Muscovites, we even had some Republicans and a couple of Americans from the Iberian thing in here, but they died a few months back, I'm afraid.'

'Are there any other Brits?'

'Two chaps from 139 squadron came up in the same transport as me, but we were separated and I have no idea if they're still alive. And there was one other poor blighter here when I arrived, but he'd been here a few months already and bought it a while back. We tend to wear out pretty quickly: nobody lasts more than eight or nine months and most end up like her in less than five,' he waved in the direction of the woman, who'd been abandoned, apparently beyond help. 'I've only been here six months or so and you can see how I am.' He laughed suddenly, the sound shocking in the quiet room. 'It doesn't matter, though; there's plenty of new "slaves" to replace the ones that die and we get a delivery every couple of weeks.'

'But only pilots?'

'Yes. Although, before the war they apparently had political prisoners and people they classified as "undesirables" doing the work.'

'Like bankers and lawyers?' Drake smiled, knowing that Askwith had been a lawyer between the wars and his family owned a bank.

'Watch it, sonny!' Askwith chuckled, shaking his head. 'Actually, I don't rightly know who they were exactly; they were all dead before I got here.'

'What the hell is Gruber playing at?' said Drake. 'Pilots aren't exactly the most physically fit or strongest of people - he'd be much better off with captives from the army and I'm sure there's a hell of a lot more than them. And while he's at it, why doesn't he just put a machine in here to do this. Whatever this is.' He frowned as he looked up at capstan. 'What the hell is it we're doing anyway? What is this for?'

'They had a bloke in here right at the start who'd been on the design team, an artistic type who had then been labelled an undesirable for some reason. He told everyone who would listen about this thing we're on. Bertha.' He spat the name, disgusted. 'We're winding the springs that power the propellers.' He patted the floor. 'There are two springs right beneath us, mounted one on top of the other. They can be removed for replacement or repair apparently, but we've never landed so I guess they don't do that very often. Anyway, they switch from one spring to the other every morning and we wind the one that's not being used until it's at full tension again. However long that takes. And if we don't finish on time they punish us.' Askwith shrugged. 'As for Gruber only using pilots, who knows?'

'Actually, Come to think of it, I might have an idea.' Drake grinned when Askwith looked at him in surprise. 'I've spoken to him quite a lot recently and I can safely say the man is a few cogs short of a logic engine, so it's probably just some ego thing - trying to prove he's the best pilot in the world or something.'

'You've spoken to him? How? When?'

'He brought me here in his private transport. He's been taken off of the northern front and reassigned to Italy. We're on the way there now.'

'Ah.' Askwith nodded in understanding. 'That explains a lot.'

'Explains what?'

He jerked his thumb at the clock on the wall over the door Drake had come through. 'For a month or so we had it fairly easy and only needed to work for seven or eight hours a day, but the last few days we've been hard-pressed to keep up, doing sixteen, seventeen, or even eighteen-hour shifts.'

'Which means that for a while they were just keeping station somewhere, but then they began to go somewhere.'

'Exactly. I just hope we get wherever we're going soon, we've been dropping like flies and the replacements aren't coming fast enough, soon there'll be nobody left to wind their bloody springs for them.' Askwith struggled to his feet. 'Come on, enough chit-chat, we should eat something then get some sleep.'

Tanya helped Drake to his feet and they followed the man as he limped slowly towards the door at the back of the room. Half-way there he glanced over his shoulder at them. 'We've got plenty of food and water, but no tea, I'm afraid.'

'Well, *that's* just not on,' said Drake. 'I'll have to complain to the manager.'

Askwith laughed. 'Same old Ace. I always liked you, I'm damn sorry the bastards got you.'

Drake chuckled, then glanced sideways at Tanya. She was limping heavily and he was supporting her almost as much as she was him. She also wasn't smiling anymore. 'You're very quiet all of a sudden. Are you alright?'

She only shrugged in reply.

'What's wrong?'

'I don't like this place; I don't know how we're going to get out.'

After they had gorged themselves on a stew that didn't taste nearly as bad as it looked and black Prussian bread, Askwith showed them around the living quarters - an extremely short tour, seeing as they consisted of just two rooms.

The main room, where they had eaten, was about the size of the room with the capstan, which the prisoners called the "winding room". It was for both eating and sleeping and was divided in two, half of which filled with long metal tables lined by metal benches and the other half by hard mats, like those used in a gymnastics class. Everything was dull grey and bolted to the floor and everything was soiled with use, but no more than the people themselves were. There were no sheets or blankets for the mats and it was not nearly as cosy as it had been in the adjacent guard room, but according to Askwith it wasn't too uncomfortable when everyone was bunched up together on the floor.

The second, much smaller, room, had two long rows of toilets out in the open with no screens for privacy and a dozen sinks with only cold water taps. Askwith told them that it was possible to wash and keep clean, but in practice most people were too tired at the end of a day's work to do more than eat and use the toilets before collapsing. However, trying to wash their clothes was impossible because there was nowhere to dry them and working in wet clothes was torture far beyond what it already was.

The tour concluded, they returned to the main room. It had only taken a few minutes, but most people had already curled up on the floor and were fast asleep, wrapped around each other like animals in order to conserve heat.

Drake couldn't help but stare as Askwith led them past the mats; there were very few men or women that didn't look malnourished, despite the plentiful food, and quite a few were trembling, though with the cold or something else, he couldn't tell. There was an almost constant chorus of coughing and wheezing accompanying the snores and sounds of soft voices coming from the people still eating.

They reached one of the few free spots on the floor. A man was already asleep there, but he stirred at their approach and smiled weakly up at Askwith who nodded in greeting.

'This is François, he was captured at the same time as I was. We look after each other and I would suggest you find someone to do the same.' Askwith eyed them and grinned. 'Although it looks like you already have.'

He lay down close to the Frenchman and looked up at them. 'Lights off is in a few minutes. Try to get some sleep, we'll be up at five, that's less than four hours from now.'

With that the man closed his eyes, rolled onto his side and was snoring in seconds.

Drake exchanged a glance with Tanya, then without a word they settled to the floor and he wrapped his arm around her, the two of them instinctively settling into one of the positions they'd slept in during their journey through Finland.

Remembering her words and the look of hopelessness on his face, he racked his brains, trying to come up with something comforting to say to her, but sleep overtook him before he got close to finding anything.

CHAPTER 14

The blaring klaxon uncompromisingly woke the pilots the next day and Askwith informed them they had half an hour to snatch some food and visit the bathroom before having to be at the capstan.

Even though Gruber had told him that they would have a tour after he'd seen to his business, nobody showed up to get Drake, so he joined the others in getting ready for the day.

Since the bathroom lacked any privacy whatsoever, the prisoners had organised it so that the women could use it while the men ate, before swapping over, but even so, Drake felt extremely self-conscious doing his business under the eyes of other men. He learnt straight away that it was imperative not to make eye contact and the best policy was to stare at a point on the floor a few feet away. Thankfully, the Prussians weren't so barbarous as to not supply toilet paper, but it was strictly rationed to a few pieces each and of the worst quality possible.

When the thirty minutes was up, the klaxon sounded again, just as insistently, and the pilots reluctantly filed out to the capstan. To Drake's initial surprise, they weren't hounded or hurried by the sailors, but then he realised that it really didn't matter if they were late starting; they would be working as long as it took to wind the spring.

Drake and Tanya followed Askwith and François over to one of the wooden bars. There were twelve bars in total with room for at least ten or twelve people at each, meaning there was more than enough space for everyone and they didn't have to worry about being split up.

Once everyone was in place, one of the pilots gave a shout, then together they started pushing, going the opposite direction as they had the day before because the two springs had been mounted back to back.

Stiff muscles from the previous day made the going slow at first, but they soon warmed up and got, if not a good rhythm, then at least some momentum going.

Once they were settled, Drake turned his head to look at Askwith, pushing beside him. He knew he should be saving his breath for the work, but he was curious. 'Most of these people look like they're not going to be able to work much longer. Why don't we slow down or let them sit and rest a bit?'

Askwith didn't have any energy to spare, despite it being so early in the morning, and he answered breathlessly, without looking at Drake. 'We tried that once, a few months back. We rotated the worst people out and took it in shifts, working slowly but steadily. It worked for a couple of days, but then we misjudged it and didn't manage to wind the spring completely. We got punished.'

'Punished? Surely that would be counter-productive? Like kicking someone when they're already down?'

'Not the way they did it.' Askwith huffed. 'Our particular circumstances give them certain creative options when it comes to punishments. The first time we didn't meet our quota they reduced the heating during the night and you can imagine it got pretty cold in here. The second time they stopped the food for the day. The third they reduced the air for a few hours - that was extremely uncomfortable, I can tell you. Even so, we wanted to keep resting the worst people, knowing they would just die if they had to work, but after that third day of missing our quota they got fed up. They ordered us to have everybody working all the time, no matter their condition, saying that next time they would just jettison the people who didn't. As you might expect, after that we did what they wanted and now we have no other choice but to work until we drop.'

Drake was rendered speechless and he remained that way because his injuries soon caught up with him and he no longer had the breath to ask questions.

At midday they took an hour to rest and most people went to get food. While Drake ate listlessly he noticed that a few people had just staggered to the mats and fallen asleep, while a couple more had just collapsed where they were at the capstan.

Askwith saw him looking and leaned close. 'They're the ones that have almost given up. It happens every time - they get so tired they can't eat, which just makes them weaker. If they make it to the mats they have a couple of days at the most. The ones that collapse at the capstan probably won't last the rest of the day.'

'Can't we do anything?'

Askwith shrugged. 'The only thing that will save them is if we get wherever we're going and stop using so much spring tension. They need rest, that's all.'

Drake's face hardened and he began to stand.

Askwith put a hand on his arm to stop him. 'What are you doing?'

'I'm going to take them some food.'

'Don't.'

'Why not?'

'Don't you think we haven't tried that? They'll just throw up anything they swallow and in the end all you'll do is make it worse for them. If you want to help them, to help any of us, the best thing you can do is keep up your strength and pull your weight. That way you take the strain off someone weaker than yourself.'

It didn't sit right with him not to help someone in need, but the last thing he wanted to do was harm them further, so Drake reluctantly tore his eyes from the unfortunate men and women and returned to his food.

All too soon the hour was up and they made their way back out to the capstan.

True to Askwith's prediction, one of the two men who'd dropped where they stood didn't get up again and was dragged away by a guard.

Drake found the afternoon to be much harder going than the morning; not only were his energy reserves completely gone, but the break had made his injuries stiffen once more. This time there was no injection from Prussian doctors to lessen the pain and it was almost overwhelming, but he nonetheless gritted his teeth and put his back into the work, determined to do his full share.

According to the clock on the wall, it was after midnight when the klaxon sounded, signifying that the spring had been fully wound, and the day ended - they had been working for about seventeen hours, if the rest periods were taken into account.

The next day came and went in a similar fashion and Drake was beginning to think that Gruber had forgotten about him, but then, at about five in the afternoon on the third day, two army guards came into the room and descended the staircase. One of the sailors pointed them towards Drake and they dragged him from his place on the bar and shoved him towards the exit.

Drake was on autopilot and for a few seconds he wasn't really conscious of what was happening. He tripped on the stairs, his legs still trying to take the short, strong paces needed at the capstan, and he only just managed to catch himself before his face hit the step. A few painful kicks from the guards woke him up to his new circumstances, though, and he grabbed at the railing, using it to pull himself up and to the top of the steps.

Waiting for him in the guard room beyond the pressure chamber was the counterfeit RAC dress uniform from the airbase and a razor. He was pointed towards the shower and told to hurry by one of the guards, who then watched while he cleaned and shaved himself.

He was ready less than half an hour later and the guards ushered him out and along the corridor towards the stairwell. He wasn't amused to see that there was indeed a lift, but he said nothing, not wanting the guards to change their minds and make him walk up the stairs.

The guards punched the button for deck nine, which he remembered held the Navy Officers' Mess, and his legs buckled beneath him as the mechanism accelerated rapidly. He threw out a hand to grab the safety rail, but before he could even grasp it, the lift was decelerating just as sharply, which took the weight off his legs and allowed him to stand straight again.

The doors opened directly into a cloakroom, and the steward, Friedrich, was waiting for them there. He dismissed the guards with a wave, before giving Drake a respectful nod. 'This way please, Lord Drake, the Generalleutnant is expecting you.'

They passed through a thick wooden door and into a lounge, which was almost as large as the capstan room in the bowels of the vessel. It was decorated in a light and airy style, as if it were a First Class Lounge on one of the Zeppelins that had flown the rich around the world in the years before the First Great War, during the golden age of airship travel - the thick carpet was Prussian grey with an interlocking cogwheel pattern picked out in gold thread and three of the walls were painted a tasteful off-white, kept bare, as if not to distract from conversation, apart from a few portraits and brass fittings for the electric lights. Even the bar was unpretentious - just a long piece of highly-polished metal along the wall in front of recessed shelves stocked with dozens of colourful bottles.

Drake barely noticed any of these things, though, because his eyes were drawn directly to the fourth wall, which was nothing more than a row of floor to ceiling windows, sloping gently outwards, providing an awe-inspiring and unbroken view of blue.

The room was filled with deep sofas and armchairs with lightweight metal frames, which were occupied by officers from all three branches of the Prussian armed forces. They were of course all wearing dress uniforms, but there was nothing of the colour, flair or individuality of the uniforms of other countries; the Prussians had "modernised" their dress uniforms a few years ago and now they were all identical across their armed forces, the only thing differentiating them the colours, which made Gruber's black dress uniform all the more unique. As the steward led him across the room he received curious looks from many of the men, but none met his gaze for very long, as if uncomfortable with his presence there.

At the far end of the room, sitting in armchairs around a glass coffee table, were the senior officers. They looked up as Drake approached and Gruber flashed him his best smile. 'Ah, Lord Drake. So good of you to come.'

Drake's mind was so numbed with exhaustion that he was almost overwhelmed by the sudden impulse to leap across the table and pummel the man. It wasn't so much Gruber's hypocrisy in thanking him for something he'd had no choice in, but rather the fact that he was apparently going to pretend that he hadn't left him to rot in the dungeons for three days and that there were men and women dying just to power his airship. Manners and social skills ingrained in him almost since birth as the heir to the Drake name served to restrain him, but he was unable to stop his fists from clenching; his boxing instincts overriding some of those more refined ones.

'How could I refuse?' He smiled coolly at Gruber, then nodded in turn to the other men around the table - the admiral, a grey-haired Italian civilian in a stylish grey suit, and an army officer in his sixties - receiving polite nods in return.

'Please join us.' Gruber waved to an armchair that had been left empty for him.

Drake took the seat and the steward leaned over him to whisper in his ear. 'Aperitif, sir? A cocktail? Champagne?'

Drake didn't feel much like drinking or celebrating, but certain things were expected in company. 'Champagne, please.'

A long flute filled with bubbling golden liquid appeared on a silver tray in front of him and he sipped from it, finding it to be a particularly good French vintage which was most likely spoils of war, as he watched the officers. With the perfunctory greetings done, they had returned to their conversation in German: a discussion of Italian politics and in particular the Prime Minister's recent declaration to follow Prussia's lead and return Italy to the glory days of Ancient Rome. While the topic of conversation didn't particularly interest Drake, the dynamic of the group did and the same social instincts that had allowed him to regain his control made him aware of the distaste that the other men had for Gruber. They hid it well, but to someone as well-versed in the niceties as he was it was plain to see. Gruber, however, was such a coarse person that he had no idea.

The polite smile that was fixed on Drake's face widened and became genuine as he realised that he had the perfect way to get some measure of revenge - he would show the man up in front of the admiral, the senior officers and his Italian ally. If it were done correctly, the man would never even realise what had happened, but it would require delicacy and tact so that he himself didn't come off as a bounder.

When the men laughed at the admiral's anecdote about the adjustments he'd had to make when he'd left his seaborne flagship behind and taken to the skies, there was a natural break in the conversation and Gruber blinked at Drake, almost as if he'd forgotten he was there. 'Oh, I'm sorry, Lord Drake. Where are my manners?' He glanced around at his fellow officers with an ingratiating smile. 'Does anyone have any objections to our speaking English for our guest?'

Drake came to a flash decision - it wasn't really of much use to him to keep his knowledge of German a secret anymore, but he could use it to fire the opening salvo in what would probably be a very one-sided war.

'Thank you for your concern,' he said in English, then paused for a heartbeat - a tiny but telling gesture that Gruber wouldn't notice, but which he was confident that the other men would pick up on and realise the significance of - before continuing in German. 'However it is unnecessary; I am actually quite fluent in your language. Please don´t trouble yourselves on my behalf.'

The other men did indeed realise what Drake was implying - that a good host would have switched languages immediately - and a hint of a smile crossed the admiral's face. Gruber, however, remained oblivious to the fact that he had done anything wrong and gaped at Drake in surprise for long seconds. 'Oh. Good. That's good. Better for everyone.'

Gruber forced a smile, then turned back to the other men, introducing a new topic of conversation as if nothing had happened.

At precisely six, dinner was announced and they made their way through double doors at the back of the lounge and into the adjoining dining room. The admiral announced, to everyone's surprise, that Drake was to be the guest of honour and he was placed at the man's right hand, displacing a somewhat disgruntled Gruber, who stalked off to the other side of the huge table in a huff.

After the modern, and frankly quite cold, lounge, the dining room was warm and inviting and had a distinctly nautical feel to it, with dark wooden tables, chairs and panels on the wall. The Prussian Navy had never really distinguished itself, but it dated back to the sixteenth century and mementos of the sailing ships of bygone eras were prevalent here in the decorations, along with paintings of maritime scenes. Like the lounge, windows took up an entire wall, but, continuing the nautical theme, they had been made to look like the stern windows of a ship and were framed with more wood.

Overall, the dining room was not nearly as impressive as the captain's state room on the Arturo, which had been a replica of the Dining Cabin of the HMS Victory, but it had a distinct, classical style, and the spectacular view of the sunset more than made up for any deficiencies.

During the meal, Gruber's complete lack of grace and table manners gave Drake ample opportunity to take digs at him and he availed himself of each and every one of them. It was the kind of character assassination he had always hated, having seen it far too often at school and university, where men and women, who had admirable qualities, were ridiculed and ostracised simply for being less fortunate in the manner of their birth, but he had no qualms doing it to Gruber.

At no point did the man become aware that he was being made fun of, on the contrary he seemed to enjoy being the centre of so much attention. Other diners cottoned on to what he was doing very early and, as the dinner progressed, Drake was delighted to see that they often contributed to setting the odious man up, offering him wine that didn't go with the course, making sure that the wrong condiments were always at hand, or simply giving him backhanded complements. Afterwards, they even provided him with the opportunity to pass the port to the right, which he took, to general but concealed merriment.

With the exception of Gruber himself, the entire mess had been in on the joke, in fact, which had made for a very jovial and enjoyable meal indeed and Drake was almost disappointed when it was all over and the officers made their farewells. There was sympathy in the eyes of most of them, but none openly expressed any opinion, instead limiting themselves to thanking Drake for, among other things, being so entertaining.

Finally, he was left alone with Gruber.

'Well!' Gruber said, rubbing his hands together in glee. 'I usually find these meals extremely dull, but that was *most* enjoyable!'

'Yes it was,' said Drake, smiling, while trying not to stare at the dried crème brûlée stuck to the side of the repulsive man's chin, which had provoked so much laughter during the brandies.

'I don't know how you did it, but I should definitely invite you more often!'

The man seemed to be proud of himself, as if he'd gotten one over on Drake by displaying him as a trophy, using his well-bred captive to advance his own reputation. Drake didn't disavow him of the notion. Instead he shook his head and grinned cheekily. 'Actually, I rather think it's my turn to play host. Shall we say tomorrow at seven, winding room three? The chef is preparing something special.'

Gruber stared at him for long seconds before breaking out into guffaws. 'Wonderful! That English sense of humour! Always laughing in the face of defeat.' He gave a short, very German bow. 'I regret that I'm going to have to decline your invitation.' He rubbed his hands and looked around the mess, now deserted apart from a few junior officers drinking at the bar and the ever-present steward, Friedrich. 'I did promise you a tour, but it's getting a little late. Perhaps next time?' He smiled at Drake's nod. 'Tomorrow then. I'm playing host to the admiral and his senior staff in my mess. You must join us to liven things up again.'

'I believe my schedule is clear, so I will be happy to accept.'

Gruber laughed again. 'Until tomorrow, then.'

He walked off and out of the mess, leaving Drake with the steward who bowed. 'This way please, sir.'

Drake followed the man to the cloakroom, where the guards were waiting, bored and half-asleep. They grumbled as they got out of their seats and took custody of Drake for the trek back down to the winding room.

Now that the excitement and the tension at being in the company of high-ranking enemies of his country had gone, the adrenaline that had kept him going completely dissipated and Drake's exhaustion made itself felt once more. He dozed on his feet during the ride in the lift and was barely aware of getting changed in the guards' room, before being shoved into the winding room. It wasn't until he was shuffling across the winding room towards the faint light coming from the bathroom and a couple of shadowy figures appeared from nowhere in front of him that he jolted back into full awareness.

'What...? Who...?'

One of the shadows lunged towards him and, before he could react, a body hit him and a hand closed over his mouth. He fought, trying to shout for help, but then he recognised Tanya's soft voice, hissing in his ear.

'Rudy, it's just me!'

He immediately stopped struggling and after a few seconds the body against him relaxed and the hand moved from his mouth. 'Bloody hell, Tanya... What are you doing here? Who's that with you?'

'It's just me, Drake, old boy,' said the second figure in Askwith's upper-class accented voice. 'Have a nice evening?'

'Super, thank you.'

'Jolly good. Well, you can tell us all about it over breakfast.' He reached out to pat Drake on the arm. 'Just wanted to make sure you got back in one piece and that they hadn't thrown you overboard yet.'

'You could have done it without scaring me half to death.'

'And where would be the fun in that?' Askwith chuckled softly. 'Goodnight, Ace.'

''Night, sir.'

Askwith wandered off and his silhouette appeared briefly in the doorway as he went into the room.

Drake waited a few seconds more to make sure he was completely out of earshot before speaking. 'Um, I'm not struggling anymore, Tanya.'

The Muscovite woman hadn't released him after stopping him from shouting out and her body was still pressed up against his, her arms around him.

She chuckled softly. 'I know. I don't care.'

Drake found his eyes had adjusted to the weak light and when he leant back and squinted at her he was surprised to find a wide smile on her face instead of the downcast look she'd had for the past couple of days. 'You look better.'

She nodded. 'I have decided not to be unhappy, because that would just be letting them win.'

Her hands moved, one going up to cup the back of his head and he found his head being pulled forwards. His lips met hers and his breath caught in his throat as she kissed him deeply, but then he jumped as her other hand reached its, much lower, destination and squeezed.

'I say, steady on!'

'Stop being so British for a while and just kiss me!'

'Yes, ma'am!'

Drake laughed quietly, but then couldn't help yelping in alarm as she dragged him to the floor and began tearing at his jumpsuit impatiently.

Their coupling was quick, but neither of them had energy for anything more. It had been more than satisfactory, though, and they were both beaming as they made their way hand in hand to the spot on the floor next to Askwith, where they instantly fell asleep in each other's arms.

CHAPTER 15

The next morning Drake was even more tired than usual due to the late night, but he made his way uncomplaining to the capstan with the others, the memory of the fun he'd had at Gruber's expense and his newfound feelings for Tanya sustaining him.

There was a surprise in stall for him, though, because as soon as he got into position, the sailors guarding them came over and shouted at him step away from the capstan.

Drake shook his head and readied himself to push, but one of the guards pushed his way past Askwith and Tanya and dragged him out by the collar.

'By order of the Generalleutnant you will not work today; he wants you rested for dinner.'

Drake blinked at him, for a moment wondering if he'd fully understood the man's German; his accent was thick and unfamiliar to him, but when the man pointed towards the living quarters it became obvious that he had. He shook his head and smiled. 'It's fine, I can work. It won't be a problem.'

He started to go back to his place, but the two guards grabbed him and frogmarched him away from the capstan.

He looked back over his shoulder, trying to see his friends, but couldn't find them in the sea of faces watching him and had to turn away from the resentful faces of men and women who were much more tired than he was, but would have to work while he spent the day idle.

One of the guards hovered around outside the living quarters, making sure that he didn't come out, but instead of resting, Drake did as much as he could to clean the space and get food on the tables ready for the men and women outside. He didn't think it would do much to reduce any bad feelings they might have towards him, but it assuaged his own shame somewhat.

After lunch, the guard once more made sure he stayed in the room and it was no surprise when again he was taken away at five o'clock and told to shower and change.

They again took the lift and this time Drake was prepared for the sharp acceleration and braced his legs.

They stopped briefly at deck six to take on board a few naval officers in dress uniforms, some of whom he recognised from the previous night. They greeted Drake cordially, but didn't engage him in conversation and when they reached the fourth deck, they filed out without another glance.

The lift didn't open directly into this mess, but rather into a small antechamber - a bare metal room with two doors leading off of it. The one to the right apparently led to briefing and ready rooms, but, unsurprisingly, they were all going to the one directly ahead, which had "Pilots' Mess" stencilled on the wall next to it.

There was no cloakroom, instead the thick bulkhead door led straight into a single huge room that combined both lounge and dining areas. Like the naval mess, it was brightly lit by floor to ceiling windows, but the similarities between the two spaces ended there because, while the other one had been tasteful and understated, the lounge a haven for convivial socialising and the dining room a place for pleasant meals in pleasant company, this mess was exactly that - a *mess*, a chaotic assault to senses.

Drink had obviously been flowing for a while and voices were raised everywhere, competing with the group of naval officers gathered around a piano at the far end of the room, belting out some kind of German sea shanty at the top of their lungs.

The area immediately around the bar to his left was populated by pilots and Drake was interested to note that there were now fifteen Crimson Barons - a full complement. They had been drinking heavily, but he couldn't tell if they were celebrating with the new arrivals or commiserating with them.

There was a tree in the corner near the piano and festive decorations had been put up, but they were strewn around haphazardly over every surface, as if Father Winter's workshop had received the same treatment as the hangars on the Finnish air base. A few of the more unsteady officers had appropriated some of them and wore strands of tinsel as scarves or belts, but the young man standing on a chair and conducting the men at the piano had been far more inventive and had added gold tinsel to his shoulder boards as imitation rank insignia and a multitude of shiny baubles to his chest as medals.

All that wasn't particularly unusual, though; similar behaviour could be found in any mess of any fighting unit around the world, rather it was the more permanent decor that gave the impression of clutter and disorder.

Only a few days before, he'd wondered if the Barons had a permanent base where they kept their trophies and he now had his answer. However, while most squadrons limited their decorations to pieces of destroyed aircraft and the occasional photograph of pilots, current and past, here signs of Gruber's narcissism were everywhere - colourful promotional posters for Gruber's many flyvies and for exhibitions of the Barons, both prominently featuring Gruber's smiling face, were hung on every wall. They were outnumbered by the more traditional trophies, but only barely - it was a good thing that the Barons had such a long history of victories.

Friedrich appeared and took custody of Drake from the guards, then led him across the room. Their progress through the crowd of tipsy officers was necessarily slow in order to avoid collisions, which gave him plenty of time to peruse the trophies in passing.

There was no discernible order to the objects on display. A tailplane with Spanish Republican insignia was next to a section of a wing decorated with Muscovite cogs and piping. A ragged and torn, canvas-covered Polish aileron was flanked by a nosecone from an early Spitsteam variant. Every country that the Prussians had come up against was represented in some way by the remnants of twisted machinery hanging from the walls, much of it antiquated and inadequate: a testament to exactly how unprepared most of the nations had been for the invasion.

However, nowhere, not even in pride of place over the bar, were Misfit trophies in evidence.

Drake had no time to puzzle over the mystery, though, because Gruber had stood from where he'd been sitting - on his own in an isolated armchair across the room, which was obviously his seat - and was approaching, drink in one hand, the other extended and movie star smile firmly in place.

'Lord Drake, so good to see you again.'

Drake shook his hand and smiled, trying to ignore the clamminess. 'Thank you for having me. Merry Midwinter.' He looked around, gesturing vaguely at the colourful decorations in order to distract Gruber while he wiped his hand on his trousers, but barely managed to keep a straight face when he caught sight of a sprig of mistletoe that some wag had hung above the man's armchair.

Gruber tutted and shook his head. 'None of that "Enlightenment" nonsense, please. Here we celebrate good old-fashioned Christmas.' He chuckled. 'Although I will forgive you if you didn't get me a gift.'

'I'm not exactly expecting one from you either.'

Gruber tilted his head in acknowledgement and took a deep draught of his drink. He smacked his lips loudly and smothered a belch, before speaking again with a voice that was hoarse from the alcoholic content of the glass. 'The admiral is running slightly late, so dinner will be delayed a few minutes - we're approaching our assigned coordinates and he's reporting to the locals over the radio or something.' He shrugged, as if such matters were beneath him.

'No need to apologise, I'm in no hurry to return to my quarters.'

Gruber smirked. 'I can imagine. Champagne?' He raised a hand and a waiter immediately appeared with a laden tray.

Drake lifted a flute from it and sipped. 'A rather impressive collection of mementos you have here for such a young squadron. There aren't many back in England who have accumulated as much as you and this isn't their first shindig.' He gazed around the room, genuinely impressed, although at the same time he was appalled at the demonstration of Prussian aggression, but then his eyes settled on a large object that was slightly out of place.

Gruber saw the direction of his gaze. 'Ah, yes. My greatest prize!' He smiled. 'Magnificent, isn't it? Care for a closer look?'

Drake nodded and they moved across the room through the crowd, which opened up in front of Gruber as if repelled by him.

A few yards from the end of the bar was a model of the airship. Fully twenty feet long, it was almost as impressive as its real-life counterpart.

Drake hadn't been able to properly appreciate Bertha on the approach and he took the opportunity to do so now, bending close to take in details that it would be impossible to see unless it was on the ground, memorising as much of the design as he could, in case he could pass on the information later. 'It's extraordinary, yes. Your engineers have created something very special.'

He wasn't just being polite; despite its size, the airship was pleasingly proportioned and it was awe inspiring in its majesty. It was just a shame that it was being used to carry such a repugnant man on missions to kill men and women who were only trying to defend their countries.

'Believe it or not, that is a working model.' Gruber said.

Drake looked up from his inspection of the lower decks and flat keel of the airship in surprise. 'This thing flies? Really?'

'Oh yes. The designers built it as a proof of concept. We don't fly it, it's too valuable for that, but when the Kaiser visited he wanted to have a go, so we took it up to the flight deck.' Gruber chuckled wryly. 'He crashed it, of course.' He pointed to the bows of the model. 'We didn't have the tools or time to repair it properly, so if you look close enough you can still see the damage the man did.'

Drake bent to look and indeed found a few deep scores in the metal that had been covered with paint but otherwise left untouched.

He straightened and stood back to take in the model as a whole once more. He idly wondered whether Hamleys would ever try to replicate it and what it would cost if they did. He was sure, though, that no matter how expensive it was, there would always be someone, some enthusiast, who would buy one. He briefly amused himself by imagining the diorama that old Mr Dunne would create, perhaps having Bertha under dogged attack by Misfit Squadron aircraft, and he fervently hoped that one day that battle would take place in real life.

He turned to speak to Gruber, but found that the man was no longer there. He frowned and looked around, eventually spotting him across the room, speaking to the admiral. The man had wandered off without saying anything - the height of bad manners.

The dinner wasn't nearly as enjoyable as the previous night's had been. With the admiral as just a guest in the mess and Gruber playing host, there was no way to politely stop the man from telling anecdote after anecdote of his life in Hollywoodland. The stories weren't particularly amusing, they were just excuses for him to let them know how many of the major movie stars he knew, although Drake did get the impression that none of them were particularly good friends with him. To cap it all off, Drake had already decided that he wasn't going to call attention to the man's deficits again; they had been seen by one and all and it would have been crass to go through the whole rigmarole again, so there wasn't even that to distract from the tedium.

Gruber seemed to think the dinner had been equally successful, though, and he was beaming when he said goodnight to his guests one by one a couple of hours later, not conscious of the fact that the admiral, and the few naval officers who hadn't drunk themselves into insensibility, had left as soon as was socially acceptable.

Finally it was just the two of them, the ever-present steward, and a few pilots still knocking back drinks at the bar as if there was no tomorrow.

'Right then! I promised you a tour and you're going to get one!' Gruber was flushed with more than just his success and he laughed as he swaggered slightly unsteadily towards the door.

Drake exchanged a glance with the steward, then hurried to catch up.

They went up to the flight deck then through a pressure chamber and into one of the rooms that were adjacent to the hangar. It was a design room, with a large worktable in the centre that had various Balsa wood models on it and several drafting tables. A plate glass window directly opposite the door gave a view over a workshop that had a line of aircraft in various stages of completion.

Gruber gestured to the window. 'This is why I took so long to call for you - I needed to make sure that my new aircraft was under construction before I could turn my mind to more pleasant matters.'

Drake wandered over to the window and peered into the workshop. The large space was narrow, no more than fifteen yards wide, only a few yards more than the wingspan of a single-spring fighter aircraft, but stretched back a good hundred. There were eight aircraft being put together inside. Seven of them were easily recognisable as Blutsaugers, but the eighth, the closest to the window, was different - a copy of the aircraft which had shot down Drake.

'Hölle behaved very well, even against the Misfits so I am giving her a chance to live again.'

'From what I saw of her, she was a wonderful machine. My compliments to her designers.' Drake nodded at Gruber, but, as the man's machine was actually heavily based on Wasp and Dragonfly, both aircraft designed by Abby Lennox and her late sister, he wasn't really paying his respects to him.

'Thank you.' Gruber, of course, hadn't cottoned on and nodded graciously. 'Well, the rest of the ship is fairly boring, all machinery and stuff, and you've seen the flight deck, so let's head back down for another drink.'

They went back down to the mess but, instead of staying there for the promised drink, Gruber crossed the now-empty room and took him through a concealed door at the back. Beyond was a short corridor with several doors leading off it, a few of them open, revealing comfortable bedrooms. In one, Drake spotted one of the Barons, insensate with drink, being ineptly helped into bed by a couple of friends, who were almost as intoxicated. The two men unsteadily straightened to attention as their commander passed, their unfortunate companion dropping off the bed and onto the floor because of their inattention. Gruber didn't so much as glance in their direction, though, he just continued to the end of the corridor and went straight through a wooden door with a brass plaque on it, inscribed with his name and rank.

Gruber's private lounge was large and comfortable. It was decorated surprisingly tastefully, in a clean and very American style, like a mansion in Hollywoodland, with carved wooden furniture and intricate brass and coloured glass fittings.

The steward was waiting for them beside a small bar and he hurried over, carrying a tray with a couple of glasses on it, one of which Gruber took automatically without looking at him. Drake shook his head when the tray was offered to him, though; he would pay a heavy price at the capstan for any sorrows drowned.

Gruber led the way to a desk at one side of the room and Drake was surprised when he saw the map of Italy spread out on it, a tiny model of the airship marking its location, not far off the east coast of Sicily - the man was evidently supremely confident that his prisoner would never be able to use the information.

'Early tomorrow morning we reach our holding position.' He tapped a spot over the water, a dozen miles or so from Syracuse, and grinned. 'That means you'll have things a bit easier in the winding rooms for a while.'

'That's nice to know.'

Gruber ignored Drake's comment and continued, holding his glass out to the side for the steward to refill. 'From here we'll launch our assault on Malta.' He dragged his finger south-west to the tiny group of islands, then scratched at it with a ragged nail. 'It's being defended by a tiny force, but the incompetent Italians are nonetheless having great difficulty subduing it and have asked for my help.'

Gruber gave Malta a last scratch, leaving the map scarred, then looked up at Drake. 'It shouldn't take more than a day or two to blow the RAC out of the skies, then the naval forces will move in and...' He gestured vaguely at the coast of Africa, only a few hundred miles beyond. 'But that is of no concern to me; the Kaiser has promised me a month or so off and I plan to go skiing in the French Alps.'

He tossed back the contents of his glass, then slammed it down on top of the Barons' next objective and spun on his heels. 'Come on! I think you'll like this.' He waved and stomped off towards the back of the room, past a white grand piano and to a door, concealed behind a red velvet curtain.

He paused, waiting for Drake to catch up and grinned. 'Ready?' Without waiting for an answer he threw the door wide and motioned for his guest to go in.

Drake raised an eyebrow, wondering what the man could think was so special - it was probably filled with his memorabilia, perhaps movie awards, or even, he shuddered to think, mementos from the many female conquests the more disreputable newspapers reported he'd made.

He was surprised to find none of those things inside, but the more he saw of the actual contents, the more he wished he had.

The large room was divided in two roughly equal halves. The part closest to the door was filled with items relating to Misfit Squadron - there were sketches and blueprints of the aircraft as well as models unmistakably purchased from Hamleys, photos of all the pilots, both official and culled from newspapers, dozens of newspaper clippings in several languages and the trophies from the aircraft Gruber had shot down, including the panel from Wasp, which Drake had expected to see in the pilots' mess.

The items dealing with the squadron in general were far outnumbered, though, by those that were at the far end of the room and which dealt with just a single one of their pilots - Gwen. They weren't, however, limited to what was widely available, but included things of a much more personal nature.

Her face was everywhere, clipped from newspapers and magazines and culled from what looked like private photos. Interspersed among them were articles dating back more than a decade and report cards from her school and university. He even thought he spied a pile of clothing in a corner, but he hoped that he was mistaken.

Drake turned to Gruber for an explanation, but the man didn't see him; he was too busy staring at one of the photographs, the official one of Gwen in her uniform after she'd joined the RAC, the same as was in every pilot's file. 'I fought against the Misfits in France, then over Britain and now over Muscovy. It seems as if we are destined to keep meeting, to be eternally circling each other, the fate of the world in just our hands. But it wasn't until Gwen Stone joined them that I felt truly challenged... Who was it that said "know your enemy"?'

'Sun Tzu, but there's more to the quote than...' Drake said, but Gruber wasn't listening and continued speaking over the top of him as he made his way over to a small table to one side of the room near another door, where a few browned and rumpled newspaper clippings were laid out for him. There were also a few typed sheets of paper and Drake caught a glimpse of what looked like the British parliamentary crest on them before Gruber shifted the newspaper articles to cover them.

'I've painstakingly collected every piece of information available about Officer Stone since she joined the Misfits. She's so much more than just a pilot, though, and that's not nearly enough to get an idea of who she really is, so I have men trawling through stacks of old newspapers for mentions of her.' He waved to the clippings. 'You wouldn't believe the amount of times she appeared in the press as a child! I have reports of conferences she attended with the photographs to match, notifications of awards at school and university, and there was even an entire article in the New Aviator dedicated to her after she took her first flight.'

He turned away from the table and took a small handheld projector from a shelf, one that reproduced movies from the portable cameras that had gained in popularity over the last decade or so. It was the type which incorporated its own small screen, less than a foot across, and when Gruber wound the handle images started to flicker on it. 'I also have this.'

The quality was surprisingly good and as Gruber held it up by its pistol-grip for him, Drake bent forward to peer at it. 'Is that...?'

'As far as I can tell, this is the only appearance of Gwenevere Hawking on film.'

Gwen was smiling broadly as she looked into the camera and waved. She was young, only a year or two older than when he'd known her. She was with her parents and all three dressed in their Sunday best, but were without shoes, standing as they were on tatami mats within a Japanese-style building, in front of a huge painting depicting a crane in flight across a cloudy sky.

The scene lasted something like twenty seconds, then blacked out. There was a whirring noise as the thin film strip was taken back to the beginning by the machine, then it began again.

'This is footage from a *Société Aéronautique* conference in Kyoto in 1927, shot by a Prussian aviation enthusiast. I forget his name. She was nine at the time and it was the first time she addressed the society as a whole.' Gruber shook his head in wonder. 'I've never come across anyone like her. The Misfits were falling apart before she arrived. They were no rival to us in France and we barely suffered any losses to them, but then over Britain...' He sighed. 'She is special. Oh so special...' Gruber trailed off his eyes fixed on the movie as it played over and over.

'You sound like you're in love with her.'

Gruber's face suddenly twisted into an expression of such hatred that Drake had never seen on the silver screen, not even when the Prussian actor had been playing the villain. 'No! Never!'

As quickly as it had appeared, the expression was gone and Gruber sighed again, dropping his head, then went on, as if Drake had never spoken. 'All this information and I *still* don't understand her,' he busied himself putting the projector back in its place. 'Which is why you're going to tell me everything you know about her.'

For a second Drake was struck speechless by the nerve of the man. 'And if I refuse?'

'That would be in nobody's best interest. Least of all Praporshik Guseva's.'

Drake opened his mouth, intending to say something like *you wouldn't dare*, or call him a name, but stopped himself just in time; that was too melodramatic, too much like one of the obnoxious man's awful movies. Instead he said nothing and just let his eyes and the hatred in them speak for him.

Gruber laughed. 'You are reluctant to carry out what you perceive as a betrayal of your friend, I wouldn't expect anything else. However, I assure you it is no such thing. After all, what possible use could I make of the kind of personal information you could give me?'

When Drake began to answer, Gruber held up a hand to forestall him. 'I don't need your answer right away. I doubt I'll be seeing the Misfits for a while because by the time they find out I'm here it will be too late for them to respond. I'll be busy for the next days, possibly weeks, so think about it.'

He glanced at the steward, who Drake hadn't noticed hovering in the doorway, and the man came over gave a small bow. 'This way, sir.'

Drake nodded politely to Gruber, but the man had already turned back to the press cuttings and didn't see it.

CHAPTER 16

The guards collected Drake at the door to the Barons' mess, but Drake barely noticed them; he was too busy brooding over Gruber's "request" for information about Gwen.

It wasn't as if he had much knowledge of Gwen that could damage her, if any; as he'd told the man before, they'd been friends as children, but had lost. However, it seemed that the man wasn't satisfied with that, or at least the man's *obsession* wasn't satisfied with that, and it wasn't likely to be until he was sure that he'd gotten every little tidbit out of him.

He'd already half resigned himself to working at the capstans for the rest of his life, forced to help Gruber and the Prussians, but this was a step too far. He toyed with the idea of refusing to work and getting himself thrown out of a hatch; better a quick end than a slow decline until death. However, it was unlikely that Gruber would allow that and with the threat of harm to Tanya being held over him he wouldn't even attempt it.

He sighed; there was really no option but to give the man wanted and hope that he wouldn't be able to glean something useful from it.

By the time they got down to winding room three there were only two sailors still awake, yawning while they played cards. The guards shoved Drake towards them, then left, laughing.

They rose to take custody of him, but he knew what was expected of him and went straight to the bathroom to get changed, eager to get to sleep.

Five minutes later, the sailors bundled him into the pressure room and began the laborious process of sealing one door, then crossing the room to unlock the next. Drake tried not to follow their conversation, but it was impossible in the confined space and he was forced to listen, disgusted, as they spoke about how the last woman who couldn't work, a Pole, had begged for her life before they'd thrown her off the airship.

There was a clunk and a slight hiss as the door opened and the guards motioned for him to go through. Their attention was fully on Drake, so they didn't see the two ghostly figures appear outside the door and they never did.

Tanya was the first in and she took the man furthest from the door, crushing his windpipe with a single blow and then holding him and lowering him gently to the floor as his face slowly darkened from lack of oxygen. She was followed by a big man, who Drake recognised as one of the other recently arrived Muscovites, a bomber pilot captured on the southern front. He moved far quicker than a man of his size reasonably should be able to and wrapped his arm around the other guard's neck. The unfortunate Prussian clawed at his assailant's arm ineffectually, his eyes bulging as the life was squeezed out of him.

It was over in seconds and then Tanya stalked towards him.

He couldn't help but flinch as she grabbed his arm and began pulling him towards the door and the darkness beyond.

'Are the other guards awake?' she asked with some urgency.

'What?' Drake blinked at her, not understanding.

She sighed in exasperation. 'The other guards in the outer room, Rudy. Are they awake?'

Drake shook his head. 'I didn't see them, I think they're asleep.'

Tanya nodded in satisfaction and spoke to the big Muscovite, who grunted and gave the limp Prussian in his hands a final squeeze before letting him tumble to the ground.

Drake paused in the doorway and turned to stare down at the two dead men. 'Wha...? Why?'

'Stop gaping, Ace and get out of the bloody way, we don't have much time.'

The voice in his ear startled Drake and he spun around to find Askwith just outside the door with François beside him. In the dim light he could just about make out a crowd of people waiting on the stairs behind them.

'What the hell...?'

'Just shift your arse and come out here with me, there's a good chap, I'll explain everything once things are moving along.'

Drake stepped through the door and hurriedly flattened himself against the railing to one side with Askwith as four or five men and women hurried past him into the room. After a moment, Tanya joined the two of them. She was laden down with supplies from the lockers within the pressure room, including masks and insulated clothing. The others soon came back out carrying more equipment, including a pair of glidewings which they gave to Tanya, and the two bodies, which they began stripping of anything useful. Once they were clear, François and the other men and women surged forward to crowd into the room and once it was full to capacity they closed the door after them.

Drake was left momentarily blind in the sudden darkness, but from the murmuring he could tell that there were more people on the stairs - it seemed like every single one of the denizens of the winding room had been there waiting for him.

He turned to Askwith, or at least towards where he thought the man was. 'I thought you said there was no escape from here!'

'No, my dear chap, what I actually said was that nobody *had* escaped from here, not that it wasn't possible. We've had a plan for a long time, based on the information that man gave us, but no opportunity to carry it out. You see, the whole plan relies on knowing that the guards are going to open the doors during the night, when they're not expecting anything, but they've had no reason to do that until you arrived. Gruber toying with you has given us the opening we need.'

Drake nodded, despite knowing nobody would be able to see him. 'That sounds reasonable, I supposed. But you,' he rounded on the presence beside him that was Tanya. 'You knew about this, didn't you? Is this why you were so, uh, well, you know, last night?'

'We had a meeting while you were gone to discuss this, so yes, I was feeling a lot happier, but what happened between us had nothing to do with that.'

'Good.' Drake smiled, relieved; he wouldn't have wanted the events of the night before to have been the result of a temporary impulse on her part - it had meant something for him and he hoped that it had for her as well. 'But why didn't you tell me about the plan when I got back?'

'Ted told me not to.'

'Sorry, old bean,' interjected Askwith, 'we couldn't risk you giving the game away.'

'You know I wouldn't talk!'

'Yes, I know, I never thought you would. But you're also a bloody bad actor. If I remember right from those skits you and the lads put on before we shipped out, you'd get all nervous and sweaty and the blighters would know something was up.'

'I wouldn't!'

'You would, Rudy.' Tanya chimed in.

'I...' Drake started to protest her betrayal, but then he remembered his poor showing during the various escape attempts and sighed. 'You're right. I probably would.'

The lights in the winding room came up slightly, just enough to see by, but not enough to take away night vision and Drake found Tanya gazing intently at him.

'What?' he asked.

She smiled. 'This time it'll work, Rudy. This time we're getting away.'

Drake mirrored her smile and opened his mouth to speak, fully intending to say something that would undoubtedly come out too soppy and that he'd probably regret later, but the moment was lost when the pressure room door hissed open and the next group of men and women began rushing in.

When the room was full the door closed, leaving prisoners still standing on the stairs, waiting to go through. There were far fewer of them, though, and Drake could see that it would only take one more trip to get them all out. However, beyond taking care of the sleeping sailors in the guard room, he had no idea what they were hoping to achieve.

He turned to Askwith. 'So, what exactly is the plan?'

'We're going to storm the other winding rooms, kill the guards and cripple the ship.'

Drake couldn't help laughing. 'Easy as that, eh?'

'Actually, yes.'

Askwith nodded earnestly and Drake blinked, taken aback. 'Really?'

'Yes. As you might have noticed, the Prussians are just a tad overconfident in their position here - there are no guards in here at night, nobody watching us, and you've just told us that the two who came with you were the only ones awake. They think they've got us safely locked away and probably don't have any plans in place for if we get out. Taking this room has been easy and we're pretty sure that we're going to be able to do the same with the others.'

'Then what?'

'Then we jettison the springs using the handy control panels in the guard rooms.'

Once again Drake found himself lost for words; it was so simple and so effective. The Prussians had unwittingly put their prisoners in the one place where they could easily do the most damage to the ship. Without its rotors it wouldn't crash, unfortunately, because its gas bags would still hold it up, but it would be at the mercy of the winds and would be forced to land.

He nodded. 'Good plan. What can I do?'

'You've already done your part, all you have to do now is make your escape when we've done ours.'

Drake glanced at the glidewings at Tanya's feet. 'I'm assuming we're going to be using those.'

Askwith nodded silently.

'There aren't enough to go around, though, are there?'

'Not even close, I'm afraid.'

'Then who goes and who stays? And who decides?'

'We took care of that last night - the only people who are going to jump are the ones who haven't been here long and are still strong enough to have a hope at surviving.' He indicated the small group surrounding them. 'That means you, a couple of Muscovites, a Norwegian, and a Pole who flew for us and was shot down over France a few weeks ago.'

'Alright...' Drake nodded slowly, reluctantly accepting the logic. It was likely a death sentence for those who stayed behind and fought, but the capstan was a living death anyway, so they had nothing to lose and all to gain and in the end they had made the choice he had contemplated but couldn't bring himself to make.

Askwith shrugged with a grimace. 'I don't like it much either, but there's nothing else to do and it's not as if it's going to be plain sailing for you either. Since we have no idea where we are and we only have your information about being on our way to Italy, the only plan we could come up with was to get to the ground in as isolated a place as possible while it's still dark and try to find somewhere safe.'

'Actually, I can help with that - Gruber showed me exactly where we are.' Drake grinned at Askwith's astounded look. 'Yes, the bad guy *did* explain the plan to the good guy just before the good guy gets away.'

Askwith shook his head. 'I swear that man thinks real life is like the movies...'

'Ah, but does he know that he is the bad guy?'

Tanya's question gave both of the men pause for thought, but then Askwith grinned. 'I'll ask him when I see him; we intend to fight our way up to the hangar and steal a cargo aircraft for the survivors.' He looked at Drake. 'So, where are we then, Ace?'

'Just off the east coast of Sicily, near Syracuse. Malta is only a hundred miles to the south west, though, and, by the look of those glidewings, I'm fairly sure they're powered - from this height the trip will be uncomfortable, but it should be doable.'

Askwith frowned. 'I'm not sure it's worth the risk, but I'll let the people who jump from the other winding rooms know that's a possibility and they can decide for themselves. I'm fairly sure most people will probably opt to go for Sicily and try their luck there, though, there might be some kind of resistance movement and they can always try to steal a boat and go to Malta that way.' He stared at Drake for a long moment, assessing him, then smiled wryly. 'You're going to try for Malta, aren't you?'

Drake glanced at Tanya, but she just shrugged as if to say it was up to him, so he turned back to Askwith. 'Yes. Yes we are.'

'I wish you luck then.'

The pressure room cycled behind them and the last of the prisoners filed into it and held the door open, waiting for Askwith to join them.

The British pilot held out his hand and Drake took it, but instead of releasing him straight away, Askwith pulled him in close. 'Let the world know we're here, let them know what the Prussians do to their prisoners.'

Drake nodded. 'I will, sir.'

Askwith smiled in satisfaction, then stepped into the pressure room. 'There will probably be an alarm of some sort when we release the springs, so we're waiting until we've taken all the winding rooms and releasing together. You'll know we're about to do it, though, because we'll reduce the pressure in here beforehand. If all goes well it shouldn't take long, so I suggest you get dressed and have your masks ready.' He winked and went to throw his weight on the door, but stopped. 'Oops. Almost forgot.' He drew himself up to attention. 'Good luck, Aviator Lieutenant Drake.'

Drake mirrored the man's posture and gave him a nod. 'Thank you, sir. You too.'

Askwith returned the nod, then closed the door.

Drake stood for a long moment, staring at it, wondering if he would ever see Askwith again.

They had never been very close; Askwith had been an old-style commander, holding himself aloof from those below him in order to maintain discipline, but he'd been something of a hero to him and the other younger officers and it had hurt when he'd gone down in France. And now he was losing him for a second time.

A hand settled on his shoulder and he turned to find Tanya gazing at him with a soft expression. She was beautiful, even with the missing teeth, still-swollen lips and bags under her eyes from exhaustion. 'He'll be alright, don't worry.'

'How will he be alright? He's aboard a bloody great airship and even if they succeed and jettison all the springs he'll still be trapped here!'

Tanya shrugged. 'I don't know. I thought that was just what you British say in this kind of situation.'

Drake blinked, then started laughing as the tension washed away from him. After only a second or two, Tanya joined him.

When Drake managed to get a hold of himself he shook his head and smiled wryly. 'This is all happening so quickly. Less than an hour ago I was contemplating my future as a Prussian slave, forced to tell Hans bloody Gruber all the useless information I know about a girl I grew up with, but now...' He reached out to stroke Tanya's bruised cheek. 'It's like a dream.'

Tanya reached up and put her hand over his. 'I know.' She smiled and swayed towards him, her eyes locked on his.

A discreet cough came from behind them and they started, the mood shattered, and turned to find the entire group grinning at them, fully prepared in Prussian-issue flightsuits, glidewings in place on their backs and breathing masks on top of their heads, ready to be put in place when the air got thin.

The two smiled at them sheepishly, then Tanya slapped Drake lightly on the cheek. 'Come on, Ace, let's get ready.'

Drake grimaced as he turned away and began to strip out of his red jumpsuit. 'Please don't call me that.'

'Why not?'

'Because it makes it sound like I'm special, like I'm better than other pilots, but I'm not.' He had been very glad when the nickname hadn't survived the disaster in France and had been content not to have one, although he had to admit he wasn't too unhappy that Gwen had resurrected her old one for him, Digger, despite how he'd earned it.

Tanya laughed.

'What? What's so funny?'

'Just thinking back to a little conversation we had in a cell a few days ago.'

'Which one?'

'The one about you being a hero.'

Drake frowned, which only provoked more laughter and he just shook his head and said nothing as he finished doing up his dark grey insulated flightsuit.

Together, they checked the glidewings, giving the springs that powered the small rotors on them a few turns to fully wind them, then helped each other heft the heavy packs onto their backs.

Finally they were ready, but then Tanya paused and looked at him thoughtfully. 'You know, I think I deserve another present.'

Drake glanced at her, amused at this return to how she had been while they had been trying to get home from Finland. When she had been full of hope. 'Another one? What on earth for?'

She shrugged. 'No reason, I just deserve it.'

He chuckled. 'So I have to pay for your teeth and buy you, how many expensive things is it now? Two? Three?'

'Five.'

Drake frowned. 'Five? Are you sure? I don't think...'

Tanya put her hands on her hips and scowled at him. 'Are you really going to argue with the woman who saved your life four times?'

'Four? Are you sure you know how to count in English?' Drake laughed. 'It would be cheaper and a hell of a lot easier just to marry you and give you half of everything I own!'

He gave her his most winning smile, the one he'd practised in the mirror so often as a child when he'd been trying, unsuccessfully, to impress Gwen. He hoped that it would work on this woman and that she would understand the unspoken question in his words.

There was a brief silence as Tanya blinked at him, scowl gone and mouth open, but then she squealed in a very feminine manner that was extremely unlike her and leapt into his arms, knocking him back into the wall next to the pressure room door. 'Took you long enough!' She kissed him enthusiastically, leaving him breathless, before pulling back and taking his hands with her calloused ones. 'Why do you think I never left you behind?'

He raised an eyebrow. 'I thought it was just for the gifts you were extorting from me.'

She slapped his face gently. 'Silly boy! I loved you from the first moment I saw you - you were like a helpless puppy, struggling through the snow.'

'Um... thank you?'

A soft hissing caught their attention, preventing any more musing on his weak showing in the forest and they grinned at each other.

'Looks like the plan's working,' said Drake.

They snatched a last quick kiss before hurriedly putting their masks on, then sat and grabbed onto the railings of the balcony, peering through them to watch the floor down below, waiting for whatever was going to happen to happen.

For long minutes there was silence as the air fled the room and, as the time stretched on, Drake was beginning to think that something had failed, that there was perhaps some backup somewhere that prevented the springs detaching while the ship was in the air. He turned to Tanya to ask if there was an alternate plan but, before he could, the klaxon blared three times, deafening in their ears and the overhead lights flashed red, so he just grinned at her instead.

The men and women on the balcony pressed their faces against the railing eagerly, unblinking and holding their breath, not wanting to miss the momentous event.

However, when it came, the release was anticlimactic; one second the capstan and the faintly marked circle was there, the next there was a gaping hole. There was no sudden list to one side as the airship lost a quarter of its propulsion, no lurch, no plunge from the skies, there was not even the expected rush of air, since the pressure had been almost completely equalised. There was just the same silence as before, but now it was tinged with a creeping cold, presaging an uncomfortable flight.

Slowly, they became aware of a hooting alarm going off somewhere in the airship as the Prussians woke to the danger in their midst and one by one the others looked to Drake and Tanya.

Faced with holding the fate of the improvised expedition in his hands, Drake felt the first doubts of the wisdom of the plan rising up, but he swallowed his nerves and stood, then led them down the stairs.

The group of men and women stood at the edge, looking down.

Far below, a solid layer of clouds shone pearlescent in the moonlight. It was beautiful, but also unfortunate; there had been no compasses with the flightsuits or glidewings because they were only for emergencies, to get people directly to the ground. They were not meant to be used to travel the kind of distance they were planning to. Drake hadn't worried about that, though, because from their height they should have been able to see the entirety of Sicily and at least part of Italy and would have been able to use those reference points to navigate. They would even have been able to see Malta when they'd gotten just a bit closer. The clouds prevented that, though.

Drake swore. 'Dammit, I was hoping for a clear night. How are we going to know we're heading the right way?'

Tanya put her hand on his shoulder and smiled. 'Don't worry, Rudy, I can read the stars. I was a sailor before...'

'Yes, yes, before the war. Right,' interrupted Drake with a laugh, his breath steaming the inside of her mask momentarily. 'Was there anything you *weren't* before the war?'

'Of course.'

Drake waited for her to elaborate, but when she didn't he chuckled again. 'Well? What?'

'A pilot,' she said simply with a shrug, as if it were obvious, then jumped.

ABOUT THE AUTHOR

Simon Brading's interest in aviation began when he was very young and at thirteen he joined the RAF section of the Combined Cadet Forces of Dulwich College with the aim of becoming a pilot. However, when he was 18, had reached the rank of Flight Sergeant in the CCF and was trying to get into a University Air Squadron, he was told that his eyesight wasn't good enough to be a pilot, so he had to move onto plan B... something else.

He tried his hand at many things before it occurred to him that he might have a few stories to tell. He never lost his interest in flight, though, and hopes to add a PPL to his very basic and probably extremely expired glider license.

www.simonbrading.co.uk

For news of special offers, upcoming releases, exclusive content, competitions and events, please follow me on social media.

Instagram - @sibrading
Facebook - Simon Brading Author
Tiktok - @SimonBradingAuthor

In addition, souvenirs and merchandise, including T-shirts, badges, stickers and more, are available from the Misfit Squadron store on REDBUBBLE at
https://www.redbubble.com/people/misfitsquadron/shop

ALSO BY SIMON BRADING

The "Displacers" series - a young adult time travel adventure series for all ages.
The Time Traveller's Nephew
The Secret of the Ancients
The Whitechapel Plot
The Price of Greed
The Time for Vengeance

The "Misfit Squadron" Series - a Steampunk series set in an alternate World War 2.
The Battle Over Britain
The Russian Resistance
A Misfit Midwinter
The Lion and the Baron
The Maltese Defence
Tales From the Second Great War
The Siege of Gibraltar
The King's Mission
The Home Front

The Dismal Futures books - stand-alone science fiction tales suitable for adults.
Empath
The Lifeboat at the End of the Universe

The "Twin Ambitions" series - ballet books for children ages 7 and up.
Fight to Dance
Back to Basics

The "Ni Hon - The Two Books" Series - a young adult series set in a dystopian future Japan.
The Black Book

Others
Public Enemy